dish

#8

Lights! Camera! Cook!

friends, cooking, eating, talking, life.

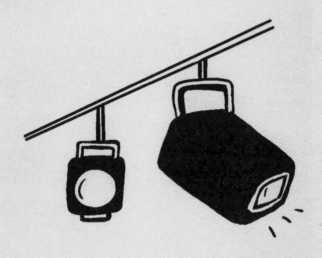

Grosset & Dunlap

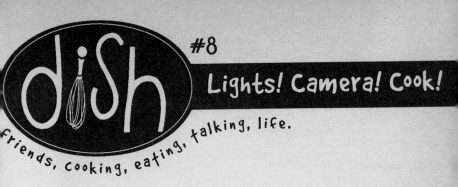

dish

#8

Lights! Camera! Cook!

friends, cooking, eating, talking, life.

By Diane Muldrow

Illustrated by Barbara Pollak

Grosset & Dunlap
New York

For Elizabeth Iozzino—D.M.

Special thanks to
Pam Griffiths and John Klindworth

Text copyright © 2003 by Diane Muldrow. Illustrations copyright © 2003 by Barbara Pollak.
All rights reserved. Published by Grosset & Dunlap, a division of Penguin Young Readers Group.
345 Hudson Street, New York, NY, 10014. GROSSET & DUNLAP is a trademark
of Penguin Group (USA) Inc. Published simultaneously in Canada. Printed in the U.S.A.

Library of Congress Cataloging-in-Publication Data is available.

ISBN 0-448-43175-0   A B C D E F G H I J

"**W**ho-oa-oah!" cried Molly Moore, pitching forward as the tip of her skate caught against the smooth ice. Stumbling, she grabbed for her twin sister's hand.

"Don't pull me!" shrieked Amanda. She struggled to stay upright.

The girls were moving too fast toward a cluster of slow-moving kids.

"Watch out!" Molly called to the kids.

Somehow, the girls managed to miss the other skaters, but now they were headed straight for a corner wall.

"*Eeeeeee!*" they screeched.

Their hands broke free from each other.

Thud! Molly's hip and upper arm hit the wall. Luckily, she'd managed to grab the handrail first, so she didn't go down. Amanda crashed into Molly, then clutched for the rail.

"*Whew,*" they said together, breathing hard. Then they began to giggle.

"I'm gonna so be black-and-blue tomorrow!" exclaimed Molly, pushing back her dark hair. "Well, at least we didn't wipe out," she added.

"And bring a bunch of people down with us," Amanda

said, wrinkling her freckled nose. She brushed the ice flakes off her velvet jeans and said, "Come on, let's get something to eat! I could really go for some hot chocolate."

The twins headed carefully toward the nearest exit, staying close to the wall as other skaters whizzed by.

"Where is everybody?" asked Molly, happy to feel the sturdy vinyl mat under her blades. She reached her hand out to help Amanda off the ice.

Amanda turned back toward the rink. Her green eyes went straight to an orange-and-white striped shirt in the middle of the rink. "There's Shawn," she said, pointing.

It was easy to find their friend, Shawn Jordan. She stood out in the crowd. Her lime-green cat glasses and bright top looked so great against her deep brown eyes and coffee-colored skin. And her flared blue jeans hit at the perfect place above her white skates.

The twins watched as Shawn waved and headed toward them, flashing a perky smile.

"Snack?" Molly called to her, pointing toward the snack bar.

"Okay," Shawn called back. She glided gracefully through a cluster of skaters and right onto the vinyl mat.

She's so cool, thought Amanda for the zillionth time. But Amanda looked pretty cool herself, with her velvet jeans, red denim jacket, and glitter in her hair. She'd tried to get Molly to dress up today, saying, "Come on, Molls, it's our class party!" But Molly had shrank back when she saw the hair glitter come out, and insisted on wearing her favorite old jeans and a ribbed turtleneck from last year. "This *is* dressy," Molly'd insisted as she put the top over her head. "It has stripes!"

"It's packed in here," Shawn commented as the girls made their way over to the snack bar. "But I just love this new indoor rink."

"It *is* fun to ice skate in April," said Molly, nodding. "It was a good idea to have our sixth-grade Celebration here."

Just then, a shrill voice called, "Yo, Shawn!"

The twins' hearts sank as they turned around to look at the rink.

The high-pitched voice belonged to Angie Martinez, Shawn's friend from cheerleading. Angie's long, sun-streaked hair flew behind her as she whizzed by with her hands on her hips. Her brown eyes flashed.

She's probably mad that Shawn's getting a snack with us, thought Amanda. *Gimme a break.*

The twins were glad to see that Shawn just shrugged and kept walking with them. Molly and Amanda had been best friends with Shawn since they were little and had helped her through some tough times—like when Shawn's mom died of a long illness.

All the twins wanted was for their friendship to stay the way it had always been. But now Angie was in the

3

picture. And Angie wanted Shawn all to herself—and was always finding ways to be mean to Shawn's other friends, especially Amanda.

And every time it happened, Shawn stayed out of it.

Amanda and Molly looked at each other and sighed. Once again, they were doing "the twin thing"—thinking the same thing at the same time.

This Angie stuff is getting old.

"A pretzel, please?" called Molly moments later at the snack bar. "And a hot chocolate?" She had to speak up over the noise of the shouts and shrieks of hundreds of sixth-graders.

"Me too, please," Amanda told the teenage girl behind the counter. "Oh, and a hot dog, too. With mustard."

"No candy bars? No ice cream?" Shawn teased her, poking her arm.

"Later," replied Amanda with a grin. Amanda loved sweets more than anyone, even more than the twins' little brother, Matthew.

"A hot dog and potato chips and a cherry soda, please," Shawn told the teenager. She turned to the twins. "Hey, where's everyone else?"

Just then, someone rushed up behind them. It was Peichi Cheng, bubbly as ever.

"Hi, *everybodeeeee!*" cried Peichi, her black ponytail swinging crazily. "I just got here! Guess what! I have huge news! You won't believe it! I'm—"

"There you guys are!" broke in another voice.

"Hi, Natasha!" cried the friends.

Natasha Ross's pale blue eyes brightened as she greeted her friends. "I thought my mom would never let me out the door! Wow, is this place *packed!*" She reached her arm over Molly's tray for one of Shawn's chips.

"Quick," ordered Molly, nodding in the direction behind them. Balancing their food, the girls tottered on their skates toward an empty table.

Peichi was almost bursting with excitement. "So, you guys, guess *what!*"

The girls looked at each other and chuckled. Peichi was so funny. She was always up, always excited about something.

"We give up!" said Molly, pulling off her navy fleece sweatshirt.

"We're going to *China!* This summer! In June for eight whole weeks! Isn't that *cool?*"

"Wow!" exclaimed the girls. They knew Peichi had always wanted to visit China.

"Yeah! We're going to visit Mom's family," Peichi went on. "We'll visit the cities of Shanghai and Beijing. Do you know how *old* those cities are? It's a really long flight—like, twenty-four hours! And we're going to visit the Great Wall of China! I can't *wait* to see that!"

"Um, what's the Great Wall of China?" asked Molly, her mouth full of chewy pretzel.

Peichi looked surprised. "Oh, it's the coolest! It's one of the ancient wonders of the world. And it's so big and long that astronauts can see it from space! It was built to keep out enemies, and it's like two thousand years old. I can't wait to videotape this whole trip! Just think, I'll get to see where my mom was born."

"That's so cool. Wasn't your dad born in China, too?" asked Natasha from beneath her shock of blonde hair. She was lacing up her skates.

"No, he was born right here in Brooklyn...Oh, hi, Angie."

The hair on the back of Amanda's neck stood up. She could feel Angie standing close behind her.

"Shawn," said Angie, ignoring Peichi, "Come back out to the ice! I want to show you how to spin."

"Okay," said Shawn, shifting in her seat. "In a minute."

"Hurry up, girlfriend." With that, Angie walked off.

"Hurry up, girlfriend," joked Molly, imitating Angie's shrill voice and sneer.

Shawn just rolled her eyes. She crumpled her napkin in her hand, then slowly stood up. "Well, I'll be back," she said, "you know, in a little bit."

As Shawn walked past the girls, they heard her sigh.

Molly spoke up to break the tension. "Well, anyway,"

Molly said, trying to ignore what had just happened, "that's so cool, Peichi. I guess Dish will have to get along without you for a while."

"That's all right," said Peichi. "Business has been slow, anyway! And it'll probably slow down even more in the summer, with people going on vacation."

Molly, Amanda, Peichi, Shawn, and Natasha—who called themselves the Chef Girls—had their own business, called Dish. Since the summer before, they'd been earning money by making meals for families in their Brooklyn neighborhood. Lots of people in Park Terrace were busy with their jobs and their kids, just like the Chef Girls' parents, and were willing to pay for some home-cooked meals to be delivered.

Sometimes the girls cooked for free, to welcome a new family, or if a neighbor was in crisis. Last summer, the family of Justin McElroy, their new classmate (and Amanda's crush), had an electrical fire in their kitchen. The McElroys had just moved to Brooklyn from Chicago, but then had to move into an apartment while their kitchen was completely remodeled.

The twins' mom had thought it would be nice to help the McElroys by making a week's worth of meals for them. With her help, Molly, Amanda, Peichi, and Shawn cooked a ton of food. That was the beginning of Dish. Since then, they'd brought in Natasha, their former arch-enemy who'd slowly become a good friend. And they'd gotten to know Peichi a lot better. It had been a real adventure—between schoolwork, music lessons, and after-school activities, the Chef Girls had made good money by cooking for big families, a school event, and even a Christmas party!

But as Peichi had just pointed out, business was slow these days.

"Maybe we should put flyers around the neighborhood," suggested Molly. "Or at least give out our business cards."

"I'll bet we have enough money right now to pay for an ad in the *Park Terrace Press*," added Peichi. She was the treasurer of Dish and kept track of the money the girls earned. After every job, when the girls got paid, they gave Peichi some money for the treasury, so that Dish would always have money for food and supplies.

"Let's just put up flyers," suggested Natasha. "It's cheaper than running an ad."

"Okay," the girls agreed.

Peichi stood up. "I'm ready to skate!" she announced. "Let's go!"

Molly's green eyes twinkled as she pointed at Peichi's feet. "Um, maybe you should put your skates on?"

"Oh, yeah!" giggled Peichi, slapping her forehead. "Go ahead, I'll meet you out there."

As the twins and Natasha stepped carefully onto the ice, Amanda's eyes went straight to Angie and Shawn. Angie had taken over the exact middle of the rink. She was gliding and spinning as Shawn and some other girls clapped. Then she stopped to teach Shawn something.

Why does Angie always have to show off? wondered Amanda. *Oh, whatever. I hope Shawn comes back home with us after skating.* Just then, she spotted a familiar head of reddish-brown hair on the other side of the rink.

"There's Justin," announced Amanda, forgetting all about Angie and Shawn. "When did he get here? Wow, he's a good skater."

Molly batted her eyes and said in a dreamy voice, "Wow, Justin, where'd you learn how to skate like that?" She couldn't help teasing Amanda sometimes.

Amanda ignored Molly and watched as Justin skillfully sliced through the crowd and came to a sudden stop near his buddies, his hockey skates spraying an arc of ice shavings.

"Let's go say hi," suggested Amanda. "Omar and Connor are there, too." She waved at the boys, trying to get their attention.

The girls had met lanky, dark-eyed Omar Kazdan and husky, freckle-faced Connor Kelly in their cooking class last summer. The boys had quickly become the class clowns—and had to be separated more than once! A few months before, while they were sidelined by the flu, the

Chef Girls had hired Omar, Connor, and Justin to help out with a big cooking job. Natasha worked with Justin on the school paper, and some of the gang shared a few classes and teachers.

But as the girls skated over and said, "Hi, guys," the boys took off, their hockey skates scraping loudly against the ice.

Natasha's mouth dropped open. She turned to the twins and said, "Did you see that?"

"Is it just me, or did those guys just totally ignore us?" asked Molly indignantly.

Amanda shrugged. "Oh, they just didn't see us, that's all," she said hopefully.

"Hello-o-o-o, Amanda," said Molly and Natasha, giggling. "They looked right at us!" Molly finished.

"No, they didn't," insisted Amanda. "Look, they're coming back this way. They'll say hi now." The three boys were skating close together, dodging people left and right.

"There you are," called Shawn, skating quickly over to the girls. She'd stolen away from Angie, who wasn't exactly the most patient skating instructor.

Shawn didn't see the boys behind her. They were coming up really fast.

"Shawn, watch out!" cried Molly. "Get out of the way!"

"What?"

Molly grabbed Shawn, and all four girls stumbled out

of the way just as the boys whooshed by, laughing loudly, without even a glance at them.

"Hey!" shouted Shawn after them. "Look where you're going!" But the boys were already on the other side of the rink.

The third time around, the boys did stop just as Peichi came skating over. "Hi, guys!" she called.

"Wanna play crack-the-whip?" asked Omar. He held out his hand to Peichi, whom the girls knew he had a crush on.

"Okay!" said Peichi happily, clueless about what had been going on.

"Don't do it!" cried Molly.

"Don't be a baby, Molly," said Connor. "Come on."

"No way. You guys are crazy."

"I'll do it," said Amanda coolly. She skated over to Justin so that she could hold his hand.

"Me, too," said Shawn.

As Molly and Natasha watched, the gang picked up a few more kids to make a long chain. Omar was at one end, and Amanda was at the other end.

Her little plan had backfired. Justin had let in Sandra, a pretty girl from his math class, who now got to hold his hand...which meant that Amanda had to hold Sandra's hand. Fuming, she looked around and realized no one else was joining them.

Oh, no, thought Amanda. *I'm on the end! I'm gonna*

die! She'd been on the end before, and had learned the hard way that the last person always got whipped around the hardest.

But it was too late. The group began to skate faster and faster.

"Okay, *now!*" cried Omar.

Then, with a big shout, Omar and some of the boys whipped the group around. The chain of hands broke and kids went flying, including Shawn and Amanda, who were pushed with such a force that they couldn't stay up.

"*Ow!*" cried Amanda as she landed right on her behind.

Shawn closed her eyes and held her hands out in front of her face as she careened into Peichi.

"*Ooof!*" cried Peichi, who fell down hard. Instinctively, she moved her hands underneath her so that no one would accidentally skate over her fingers.

"Peichi, I'm so sorry! Are you okay?" cried Shawn.

There was a pause.

"Uh-huh," replied Peichi slowly, as she struggled awkwardly to turn around. "Ouch...Are you okay?"

"I'm okay," giggled Shawn as she helped Peichi up. "You made a nice cushion!"

Meanwhile, Amanda had to help herself up. Justin was long gone with the other guys, who were still skating fast in a large group.

"I can't believe those guys!" shouted Amanda as Molly and Natasha skated over to her. "They're being such jerks!"

12

Just then, a whistle blew. A burly teenage guard skated quickly over to the boys, who stopped and huddled in a corner. All laughter and shouting stopped as everyone turned to watch.

"*Ha*-ha," sang Molly. "They're in trouble now!"

"Cut the horseplay," the guard tersely ordered the boys. "I want all of you off the ice for fifteen minutes. Come on, move it."

Omar, Justin, Connor, and some of their buddies slowly skated off the ice and went inside.

"Where's that guard been?" asked Natasha. "This is the first *I've* seen of him!"

"Yeah, it's about time he did something," said Amanda. She was still smarting from seeing Justin reach for Sandra's hand...and her buns weren't feeling so great, either.

"I've had enough skating!" declared Peichi as she and Shawn met up with Natasha and the twins in a corner of the rink. "I know I just got here, but I'm sore all over!"

"Me, too," said everyone except Natasha.

"Let's go home," suggested Molly. "My mom said you guys could come over for dinner. Do you want to?"

"I will!" said Peichi. "I'll have to call my mom first. What's for dinner?"

Everyone giggled.

"I don't know," said Amanda. "But whatever Mom makes will be good!"

"I can come, too," said Natasha as the girls skated over to the exit. "And I don't even have to call first, 'cause I told my mom I might go to your house afterward." She smiled. "I had a feeling you'd have us over."

"Good! What about you, Shawn?" asked Amanda.

"Well, Angie sort of already invited me to her house. I wish you'd said something about it sooner."

Amanda faced Shawn and said, "I didn't know you needed an invitation to come to our house. You practically used to live with us."

"I'm sorry, you guys," said Shawn. "I'll call you tomorrow." She stopped at the exit, because Angie was still on the ice, calling, "Hey, Shawn!"

"Bye," said Molly to Shawn. "See you later."

"Bye," said Shawn. "Bye, Manda."

"Have fun," was all Amanda could say. As she went inside, she began to feel a strange coldness...and it wasn't from landing on the ice.

She didn't feel sad, and she didn't feel angry.

She didn't feel anything at all.

Maybe I don't care about Shawn anymore, she thought. *That's horrible!*

chapter 2

"**...E**arth to Amanda!" Peichi was calling. "Hello!"

"Huh?" said Amanda, looking up from unlacing her skates.

"I said, 'What kind of role do you have in the spring play?'"

Amanda blushed. She didn't realize she'd completely spaced out.

The thought of the play cheered her up.

"Oh," she said, "it's gonna be fun! I get to play the part of Lady Peacock. I'll wear a long yellow evening gown and a cool feather boa! *And* a big diamond tiara!"

"Really?" asked Natasha. "That's cool."

"Actually, I don't know what I'm wearing yet, but that's what the actress who played the part in the movie wore. The play is a mystery that takes place in a big old mansion. It's called *And Then There Was One*. I get to speak with an English accent again! Isn't that cool?"

Molly rolled her eyes. "She's gonna speak in that accent all the time at home, just like she did during *My Fair Lady*," she groaned.

"I hope I get to write the article about the play for the paper," said Natasha. "Does it have as big a cast as the Autumn Dinner Theatre Musical?"

"No, it's pretty small compared to *My Fair Lady*."

"So it's a big deal that you got in, right?" asked Natasha. "That's great! Is your part big?"

"No," replied Amanda. She struggled with a knot in one of her laces. "It's small, but I have some funny lines. I wish I had a bigger role, but I'm just glad I made it. And maybe by eighth grade I'll get the big roles!"

"You'll be the star of Windsor Middle School!" exclaimed Peichi.

"You mean the *diva* of Windsor Middle School," cracked Molly. "She'll wear sunglasses in the halls and be like, 'Out of my way, everyone!'"

"Very funny," retorted Amanda, poking her sister in the ribs. "Hey, look, there go Justin and The Jerks. They look pretty bummed out."

"They took off their skates," Natasha pointed out. "I guess they're leaving."

"They're too embarrassed to hang out now," giggled Molly.

"Well, I'm not leaving the same time they are," said Amanda indignantly. "Let's wait until they're *long* gone."

"Hi, Mom!" called Molly as the girls trooped into the Moores' tall brick townhouse.

"*Aaaaaaaaaaaghh!*" came a shriek from the living room. "Get that thing out of this house!"

"*Ooops,*" the girls heard Matthew say.

The girls rushed toward the living room as Kitty came out like a shot, her claws scraping against the wooden floor.

There was Mom, and Matthew, chasing a hopping thing.

"What is it? What? *Aaaagh!*" screamed the girls. They huddled in the doorway.

Matthew crouched into a corner near the brick fireplace. He cupped his hand over the thing. "Got it!" he announced.

That's when Mom began to laugh. Mom had the loudest laugh.

"What *is* it?" asked Molly.

"Just a frog," said Matthew. "He jumped so high that it scared Kitty! I found him outside in the garden."

"And that's where you're going to take him right now," ordered Mom between chuckles. "Actually, he's a cute little froggie. But you know how I feel about critters in the house! I'll bet he came from somebody's backyard pond."

"But he's not really a critter, Mom," protested Matthew. "A critter is like a raccoon, or a hamster—"

"Don't remind me," said Mom, wincing. Then she looked around and said, "Hi, girls!"

Molly turned to her friends. "Mom's thinking about the time that Matthew brought a hamster home from school, and lost it in the house, and it scared Mom when she was down in the laundry room."

"I thought it was a rat or something!" explained Mom. "Matthew hadn't bothered to tell me that he'd brought a hamster *home* for the week! Out you go, Matthew. Out, out! And wash your hands when you come back in."

"Or that frog will give you warts," Peichi teased Matthew.

"Really?" he asked, his eyes wide. Then he gave her a wiseguy look. "Oh, you're just kidding. I'm not dumb." He walked through the cluster of girls, muttering, "Everyone's always telling me to wash my hands."

Mom shook her head as Matthew let the kitchen door slam behind him on the way to the garden. "Honestly! He has nicer clothes. I don't know why he insists on wearing those beat-up jeans and the same dingy T-shirt day after day...Boys!"

"Yeah, *boys*," grumbled the girls.

"I need a sweatshirt," announced Molly. "It's getting chilly out there, Mom. I think it's going to rain." She'd come in from the garden, where the girls were hanging out, beading necklaces and listening to the radio. They'd turned it up pretty loud, to avoid hearing the sound of Matthew screeching away on his violin upstairs. "Can I bring out some more cheese and crackers?"

"No more crackers, sweetie," said Mom. "I'm going to make dinner now."

"What are you making?"

Mom sighed and opened the refrigerator door. "I'm not sure. There are a lot of us tonight, so I'll make pasta...but which sauce? *Hmmmm*...By the way, where's Shawn, honey? I thought she'd be here today."

"So did we," stated Molly.

"Oh." Mom's brown eyes looked concerned. "You didn't have another argument with her, did you?"

Molly shrugged. "No. She'd already told Angie that she'd go over to *her* house."

"I see. Well, how about helping me choose a pasta sauce? We could make pesto, or maybe something with the leftover salmon..." She reached for a container and inspected the contents. "Forget it, there's not enough salmon."

"I know!" cried Molly. "What's that sauce? It has a long name? With the tomatoes and the bacon in it?"

"Oh! You mean *spaghetti all'amatriciana?*" asked Mom in a perfect Italian accent. Mom knew how to speak Italian because her grandma was from Italy. Nana

Giovanna had taught Mom and Aunt Livia the language from the time they were little. When Mom got older, she spent a year in Rome during college.

"Yeah! Oh, make that, please," pleaded Molly. "You haven't made it in a long time."

"I made it two weeks ago," said Mom, pinching Molly playfully. "That's not so long!"

Just then, the other girls scurried in to escape the big raindrops that had begun to fall.

"Do you guys want to go up to our room, or just hang out here?" Amanda asked Peichi and Natasha.

"Let's stay here," said Natasha, "in the nice kitchen!"

The Moores' large kitchen was a great place to gather, with its cheerful yellow walls, bright rugs shaped like apples and pears, and Mom's collection of funky teapots. The twins loved to sit at the big table and do their homework and be near Mom. Mom loved to cook, even though she was busier and busier these days, teaching art history at Brooklyn College. Dad helped her by cooking sometimes. And he always took over the kitchen on Saturday mornings when he made his yummy blueberry pancakes.

"We can help you, Mrs. Moore," offered Peichi. "What should we do?"

"Now that you're cooking experts," said Mom, "why don't you and Amanda cut this meat into thin strips? And I'll chop an onion." She handed Peichi a flat package wrapped in white paper.

Peichi opened it and saw thin, round slices of meat. "What is this?" she asked. "I've never seen it before."

"It's called *pancetta*. Italian bacon," explained Mom. "It has a different taste than our bacon. This is a little saltier."

"You wouldn't want to eat it with pancakes," said Molly, reaching for a can of diced tomatoes, "but you'll love it in the pasta."

Meanwhile, Shawn and Angie had hung out longer at the ice-skating rink, and were finally on their way to Angie's place.

"Let's pop in to that *bodega* to get some gum," suggested Angie, who was already chewing a big wad of it.

"That what?" asked Shawn.

"*Bodega.* You know, a Hispanic deli. The one over there." She pointed to Franco Mini Market, a corner store with a green and red awning.

"Oh," said Shawn. "I like your accent when you say that."

Angie chuckled and said, "My mom makes me speak all Spanish words with an accent, or she gets mad. She wants me to speak right when we go to Puerto Rico to visit my relatives."

Shawn followed Angie into the little store, where a

radio played lively salsa music and the food on the shelves had labels printed in Spanish.

Angie walked right by the gum-and-candy display.

"There's the gum, Angie," Shawn pointed out, but Angie kept walking toward the back of the store. As Shawn followed her, she circled the store, came back up to the candy and gum, and paused. "I don't see the gum I like," she said. "Let's go."

"Which one are you looking for?" asked Shawn. She saw lots of different brands, all the ones she knew.

"Doesn't matter. Let's go."

"Well, okay," said Shawn, puzzled.

After the girls had walked another block, Angie slyly pulled an unopened pack of gum out from the pocket of her white velvet hoodie. "Would you like a piece of delicious Double Trouble Bubble Gum?" she asked.

Shawn's eyes opened wide. "Angie!" she gasped. "Where did you get that? Did you *steal* it?"

Back at the Moores' house, Natasha had offered to sauté the onions in olive oil.

"Okay, Natasha, if you want to," said Mom.

Just then, Mr. Moore strolled into the kitchen. It looked like he'd forgotten to comb his graying black hair that day, and he was wearing jeans and what Molly called his "Saturday shirt"—a faded baseball jersey he'd owned since college that Mrs. Moore constantly threatened to throw away.

"How's Matthew's practicing going?" Mrs. Moore asked him.

"Not bad, not bad," replied Mr. Moore, looking around the kitchen. "Hello, girls! Hey, something smells good. Is this a cooking job? Or will I actually get to eat this food?" He chuckled at his little joke.

"This is our dinner, Dad," said Molly. "But you have to do the dishes!"

"Fair enough," said Dad. He sat down at the table and began to flip through the *New York Times* sports section.

"Hey, Dad, I can't wait to start softball practice on Monday," said Molly, looking over her dad's shoulder. "I hope they don't just stick me out in left field—"

"*Ow!*" cried Amanda as she sat down. "I forgot—it hurts when I sit. Mom! You wouldn't believe what jerks Omar and Connor were today at the rink!"

"Don't forget Justin," added Molly with a grin.

"And Justin," said Amanda sadly.

"Yeah! They were so weird! The acted like they didn't even know us!" cried Molly.

"Really!"

"Yeah!" added Peichi. "And then guess what all three

of them did? They practically ran Shawn over! They just came barreling past us. Then they played crack-the-whip and pulverized us!"

"That's terrible," said Mom mildly.

Dad didn't look up from his paper. He seemed to be reading something *very* interesting.

"What's the deal, Mom?" asked Amanda. "They're our friends—why did they suddenly act like they'd never seen us before?"

Dad stood up suddenly. "Time to take out that garbage!" he said with a chuckle, and left the kitchen.

Mom stirred the tomatoes into the skillet with the onions, then turned to the girls and leaned against the kitchen counter. "Welcome to life with boys," she said with a smile. "Let me tell you a little secret...Boys can be *very* immature! And here's another secret. They never really grow up!"

"I heard that," called Dad from down the hallway. "Don't believe a word of it, girls!"

Everyone cracked up.

A few blocks away from the Moores' house, Shawn wasn't laughing.

"Well, *duh!* Yeah, I stole the gum," Angie was saying.

She looked at Shawn quizzically. "What's the matter? Haven't you ever lifted a pack of gum?"

"No."

"No?"

"I've never stolen anything in my life."

Angie threw back her head and laughed loudly. "Girlfriend, I never knew you were so *good*. Come on, do you want to try? It's easy...You didn't even see me make off with this."

"No, I didn't."

"That's because I'm good at it. I'll teach you."

"No thanks."

"Oh, come on, Shawn! Everybody does it. Wow, you really are a geek."

"I'm not a geek," retorted Shawn, feeling her cheeks getting hot. "I'm just not a thief like you. I'll see you later. I'm going home."

3

The following Monday afternoon, the twins ran into Shawn as they all headed down the crowded, noisy hall to the cafeteria.

"Hi," said Shawn softly. She smiled, but her eyes looked sad.

"Oh, hi," said Amanda, trying to sound casual.

"Hi, Shawn," said Molly. "Um, do you want to have lunch with us?" The girls never knew if Shawn would eat with them or with the cheerleaders.

"Sure," said Shawn. She looked relieved to have been invited. "I wonder what's for lunch today? Chili con carne for the kazillionth time?"

No one said anything, so she added, "So—did you guys have fun after skating?"

"Uh-huh," said Amanda. "We hung out, and then helped Mom make a big dinner, and then we watched a movie." Deep down, she still felt that horrible nothing feeling toward Shawn.

"By the way, we put up some Dish flyers when we went to the video store," added Molly. "So, uh, did *you* have fun after skating?"

"Um, it was okay," said Shawn. She wasn't ready to tell

the twins about Angie stealing the gum—and how that had made her want to turn and run straight to the Moores'. But the twins would have asked her why she'd left Angie.

As the girls picked up their trays and got in line, they heard Angie come up behind them. As usual, she was talking and laughing loudly.

"Oh, I almost forgot to tell you. I had a really cool day yesterday," blurted Shawn, not looking in Angie's direction. "Dad and I took the subway into Manhattan and went to the Metropolitan Museum. We looked at a fashion exhibit about the wild clothes that people were wearing in the 1960s. They had plastic dresses, paper dresses, and dresses that lit up with batteries! Pretty funny! And then we saw some of the mummies...I can't believe those old Egyptian tombs. They were like big houses inside, have you ever seen them? You've really gotta go see them. They're wild!" She laughed nervously.

The twins shot each other a look that said, *That's weird.*

Shawn wasn't her cool, collected self. And why did it seem like Shawn and Angie were suddenly ignoring each other?

After school that day, Amanda had to speak to her

science teacher after class, which made her a few minutes late for play rehearsal. She rushed into the drama classroom, her face red with embarrassment. She hated to be late, especially for Ms. Barlow, the glamorous, kooky drama teacher whom the Chef Girls had cooked for a couple of times.

"...I think it sounds like a *fabulous* opportunity!" Ms. Barlow was saying dramatically. "If you're interested," she went on, "come talk to me! You'll need to make a videotape, since there are no local auditions. I'll help you choose the right kind of material. Okay? *Great.* Now let's get started on rehearsal. We're going to work on Act Three."

The Act Three players grabbed their scripts and walked up the few steps to the drama classroom's little stage.

Amanda turned to Bruce Macmillan, who was playing the character of Detective McSweeney. "What's Ms. Barlow talking about?" she whispered. "What are we making videotapes for?"

"Spotlight Arts Camp," Bruce told her. "It's a six-week thing where you get to take acting classes, and be in one-act plays, and learn mime and tap dancing and stuff. Ms. Barlow got something in the mail about it and thought some of us might be interested."

"And you have to make an audition tape?"

"Yeah. And you send it to California, where the camp is."

Amanda pictured herself with a bunch of cool kids studying pantomime on a green hill overlooking a beautiful lake. *Summer camp, only for actors!* she thought. *That sounds like major fun.*

After rehearsal, as the students gathered up their backpacks, Amanda went up to Ms. Barlow, who was re-applying her deep-red lipstick.

"Yes, darling," said Ms. Barlow, squinting into her compact mirror.

"I'm sorry I was late today, Ms. Barlow," said Amanda. "I had to talk to my science teacher after class."

Ms. Barlow snapped the compact shut and looked up, her dark eyes twinkling.

"Not a problem!" said Ms. Barlow. "So, what do you think about drama camp? Oh, I wish I could go myself. Doesn't it sound *terrific?*"

"It does," said Amanda. "But I'd never get in."

"We'd make sure that you'd have the *best* audition tape possible. You should show those folks *everything* you can do."

"Well," said Amanda with a nervous giggle, "I'm not sure there's much I *can* do."

"You can sing well enough," said Ms. Barlow matter-of-factly, "and you know how to do two types of British accents, thanks to *My Fair Lady* and the play we're doing now. So we'll have you sing the songs you sang in *My Fair Lady*, in the costume you wore. And you can do the piece you did for your audition for this play, and of course your new scenes. Okay?"

"Thanks, Ms. Barlow," said Amanda breathlessly, swept up in her teacher's enthusiasm. "I—I'll think about it."

Amanda wasn't sure about spending a whole summer away from Molly. But just the thought of making an audition tape made her feel more like a real actress.

"Hello, Peichi? Hi, it's Amanda."

"Oh, hi! What's up? I was just reading our travel guide about China. It looks so awesome! Hey, did you think Shawn was acting weird today? And did you finish your book report?"

Amanda chuckled and shifted the phone to her other ear. "I'm still working on my book report. And, yeah, I thought Shawn seemed a little—different—today." That was all Amanda wanted to say about Shawn. Despite how difficult things had been with Shawn lately, it seemed too private to discuss with Peichi.

"Anyway," Amanda went on, "guess what! I might be making an acting videotape! And I wonder if you could help me with it, now that you're a bigshot filmmaker!"

Peichi giggled. "Yeah, that's me," she said.

Peichi had recently made a videotape documenting Chinese New Year celebrations in New York City and within her own family. When the video was finished, Peichi had held a "premiere" and had the girls over to see it. She'd had so much fun making her film that she thought she'd like to grow up to be a filmmaker.

"Anyway," Amanda went on, "I'm wondering if you can help me make my tape? And maybe you could shoot me a few times for practice, so that I can get used to being on camera?"

"Sounds good," said Peichi. "That'll be fun! Gotta go. We're having dinner now."

"Okay, we'll talk about it tomorrow," said Amanda. "Bye."

As soon as Amanda hung up the phone, it rang again. "Hello?"

"Hello, I'm calling for Dish." The woman's voice was deep and professional-sounding, like a radio announcer's.

"Yes, this is Dish. I'm Amanda Moore. How can I help you?"

"Oh, hello, Amanda. My name is Daphne Dupree. I saw your flyer at Parkside Video."

"Oh! Good," said Amanda happily.

"I'm giving a bridal shower soon," said the woman, "and I thought it would be nice to have a brunch in my garden. Can you do a brunch?"

"Sure," said Amanda. "We—"

"I mean, I can make a brunch myself," interrupted Ms. Dupree. "I'm a good cook. But I'll be on a business trip until the day before the shower. So I'll need someone to do the food while I decorate."

Amanda smiled. "I see," she said politely, wondering why the woman seemed embarrassed that she couldn't do it all.

"AMANDA! DINNER!" bellowed Matthew from the kitchen.

"Matthew, not so loud," Amanda heard Mom scold.

"Excuse me?" asked Ms. Dupree. "Does your roommate need to speak to you?"

"Er—roommate?" asked Amanda, confused. "No, that was nothing." She quickly shut the door of the den. "Anyway, what day is the bridal shower?"

There was a pause.

Oh, no, thought Amanda. She knew what a pause usually meant: a rush job!

"Well," said Ms. Dupree in an apologetic tone, "it's this Saturday. I just found out about my business trip today."

"Oh, this Saturday. Well, that should be all right," said Amanda, wincing. *Yipes! Saturday is just a few days away!* she thought.

"What will you make? This is for a colleague of mine, and it really has to be perfect," said the woman anxiously.

Amanda frowned. *Lady, you're making me nervous,*

she wanted to say. Instead, she said brightly, "How about eggs Benedict?" For some reason, that had just popped into her head...even though she wasn't quite sure what it was.

"Fabulous!" said Ms. Dupree. "That'll be nice. However, I'd prefer that you make it with smoked salmon instead of the traditional Canadian bacon."

"*Er*—not a problem," said Amanda, trying to act as if she knew what Ms. Dupree was talking about.

"And you'll make some other things, too? In case some people don't want eggs? I'd like a fruit salad, some breads—"

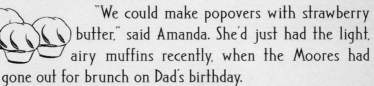

"We could make popovers with strawberry butter," said Amanda. She'd just had the light, airy muffins recently, when the Moores had gone out for brunch on Dad's birthday.

"Ter-*rif*-ic. There will be fifteen people. Thanks so much. I'll expect you at ten o'clock. 'Bye-bye." *Click.*

"'Bye," said Amanda to the dial tone. She laughed softly to herself, thinking, *Oh, well, we've had tougher jobs. I guess Dish can handle Daphne Dupree!*

Amanda joined the family at the dinner table and said, "Guess what! We have a cooking job. Finally! It's gonna be a bridal shower brunch—for a new client named Daphne Dupree. She sounds like a real big shot!"

Everyone looked impressed with the job, even Matthew.

"Great!" said Molly, helping herself to some mashed potatoes. "Let's e-mail the Chef Girls right after dinner."

To: happyface; BrooklynNatasha; qtpie490
From: mooretimes2
Re: Dish job!

Attention, Chef Girls! We got a job
b-cuz of the flyer we put up at the
video store! A bridal shower brunch
thingie! The ☺ news? We think it'll
be pretty easy. The ☹ news? It's this
Saturday, only 5 days away! ;-@
    Let's talk about it tomorrow in the
caf. OK?
    L8R,
    M&A

Meanwhile, Shawn was on the phone with her cousin Sonia, who lived down in South Carolina near Grandma Ruthie. Sonia was about to graduate from college.

"Listen, Shawn, I don't want you to worry about Grandma Ruthie," Sonia was saying. "Okay? She's in good hands here with a wonderful doctor."

Shawn swallowed hard, and a tear trickled out of her eye. She took off her purple cat glasses to brush it away.

"If you say so," said Shawn slowly. "Can I talk to her?"

"She's sleeping right now, Shawnie," replied Sonia. "Put your dad on again, and I'll call you tomorrow, okay? You can talk to Grandma Ruthie then."

"Okay. Here's Dad. 'Bye."

"Don't worry, baby. Grandma Ruthie's going to be fine," Mr. Jordan told Shawn after he'd hung up the phone.

"What does she have again?" Shawn asked.

"She has pneumonia. That's when the lungs become inflamed. So that's why her chest hurts."

"Is she really going to be all right?"

"She sure is. I wouldn't tell you that if it weren't true. I spoke to her doctor just a few hours ago. Are you okay, baby girl?"

"I'm fine. I'm just worried about Grandma Ruthie."

"Do you have any homework?"

Shawn sighed and let her head fall back onto the sofa. "Of course."

"Well, why don't you go get started then. And when you're finished, I'll make you the *biggest* hot fudge sundae you ever did see."

Shawn giggled. "Can I call my friends first?"

"Five minutes per friend. That's it."

"Okay." Shawn sighed and stood up. Her whole body felt heavy.

This week has been the pits, thought Shawn. *This had better be as bad as it gets!*

"Hi, Manda, it's me," said Shawn softly when Amanda picked up the phone.

"Oh, hi, Shawn. What's up?"

"Well, Grandma Ruthie's sick. She has pneumonia."

There was a gasp.

"Really! Oh, no. Is she okay?"

Shawn shrugged. "My dad says she's gonna be okay. But..."

"Pick up the other line," Amanda called to Molly. "Grandma Ruthie's sick."

There was a clicking sound. "Hi, Shawn," said Molly. "Is Grandma Ruthie in the hospital?"

"No."

"Oh, good," said the twins at the same time, which made Shawn chuckle.

"I can't stay on the phone," said Shawn, "'cause I have to write that book report for English. But I just—wanted you guys to know."

"Oh, Shawn," said Amanda, "I'm glad you called. I'm sure she's going to be fine."

"That's right," added Molly. "Please don't worry, Shawn. But we know what you're going through. We really do."

"You've been through this with me before," said Shawn, her voice breaking.

"We know you're thinking about your mom—" Amanda nearly whispered.

"But it's not going to be like that," said Molly confidently. "Okay? She's gonna be fine."

"Okay," said Shawn. "I've gotta go." She paused. "You guys are great, you know?"

"We know!" cracked Molly, lightening the mood. "Bye!"

"Bye," said Amanda.

"See you tomorrow," said Shawn. She hung up.

She stared at the phone, thinking about all the years she'd spent with the twins. She remembered early-morning walks to school...getting scolded together by Mrs. Moore for eating too much Halloween candy...and all those sleepovers in the twins' large room, after Mom got sick...

Brrrriiinnngg!

The sound startled Shawn. She quickly answered the phone to cut off the sound.

"Hello?"

"Hey, Shawn, it's Angie."

"Oh—hi. Um, what's up?"

"What's up with you? You sound like you're crying or something!"

"Well, maybe I was," said Shawn defensively.

"Whoa, whoa," said Angie. "What's goin' on?"

Shawn didn't say anything.

"Listen, Shawn," Angie went on. "I'm sorry I called you a geek the other day. Can we just forget it?"

Shawn rolled her eyes. "I *guess* so."

"Good."

Shawn thought she heard Angie exhale with relief. Or was she snickering?

"I just found out my grandma's sick," Shawn blurted.

"No way. Is she bad?"

"She has pneumonia...I guess you could say that's pretty bad."

There was a pause.

"I'm so sorry, Shawn," said Angie. This time her voice sounded softer. "Don't worry. She'll be okay."

"Thanks."

"Shawn, I know what you're going through. I've had hard things to deal with, too. Like...when I got held back in school."

"What?"

"Yeah, I had to—repeat fifth grade. My parents were fighting a lot then. I was upset all the time, and I missed a lot of school."

"So, you're supposed to be in—"

"Seventh grade."

"Oh." Shawn wasn't sure what to say next.

"You don't know what it was like," said Angie simply. "It was really hard to know I couldn't move ahead with my friends. And then those friends...weren't my friends, really, the next school year. You know what I mean? I begged my mom to let me switch schools so I could start over, with people who didn't know. You're not gonna tell anyone, are you?"

"Don't worry, Angie. I won't tell anyone."

"Okay."

"I have to go study."

"Shawn? I really hope your grandma gets better soon, okay?...'Bye."

Shawn smiled. "Thanks, Angie. 'Bye."

Wow, thought Shawn as she hung up the phone. *Angie got held back! I'm not the only one who's been through some tough stuff. I just wish my other friends knew the "real" side of Angie. Too bad Angie doesn't let everyone see it.*

chapter 4

"Hi-eeee!" said Peichi to the friends as she set her crowded tray down on the table the next afternoon. "Hey, Justin and Omar are right over there. They're looking over at us. What should we do?"

"Really?" asked Amanda, looking cautiously in the boys' direction.

"Ignore them," said Molly.

Amanda quickly turned back to her friends. "Yeah, ignore them," she echoed. "We've got business to discuss, anyway." She pulled out a recipe from her backpack. "Like eggs Benedict!"

"What's eggs Benedict?" asked Elizabeth, slipping into the empty seat near Shawn. Elizabeth Derring was new to Windsor Middle School. She and her Aunt Paula had just moved from Minnesota into an apartment in Natasha's large house. Petite and cute, with deep blue eyes and wavy auburn hair, she was a talented cheerleader. The Chef Girls liked her, though as a group they hadn't hung out with her much yet. Elizabeth had been quick to make friends with other people, too, and had joined the debate club.

Amanda scanned the recipe. "Well, an English muffin is on the bottom—"

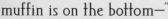

"Then you put Canadian bacon on top of that—" Molly broke in.

"But our client wants us to use smoked salmon instead," Amanda interrupted. "And then you put a poached egg on top of the meat, and hollandaise sauce on top of *that*."

"Don't you guys think it'll be perfect? Plus we could make popovers with strawberry butter," said Molly.

"It all sounds great," said Natasha, reaching for the recipe. "Hollandaise sauce," she read aloud. "This goes on top of the eggs? I think I've watched my mom make this. It's kind of tricky, but I think we can handle it."

"We should practice making it," suggested Shawn.

"Yeah, but when?" asked Molly. "It's already Tuesday. It really should be today, because I don't have softball practice. The coach is sick."

The girls looked at one another.

"Right after school? At our house?" suggested Amanda. "Today's the one day this week that none of us has any school activities."

"Oh, yuck!" cried Shawn suddenly. Her hand flew up to her neck. "Who's shooting spitballs over here?"

The girls heard loud laughter and turned to look in the direction of the boys' table.

"Don't look over there!" Molly whispered. "*They* did it!"

"Yeah!" agreed Natasha. "Let's ignore them!"

Amanda chuckled. "That's gonna drive them crazy," she

said. "Like, if I ignore Matthew when he tries to bug me, he almost goes insane!"

The girls laughed, but then Shawn's face quickly grew serious.

"Are you going to talk to your grandma after school, Shawn?" asked Natasha softly. Shawn had told her and Peichi the news earlier, before school started.

"Uh-huh," said Shawn. She looked at the twins. "And then I'll come over to your house." She smiled. "We have a menu to plan!"

Amanda smiled at Shawn. That coldness she'd felt toward her friend was long gone.

What a relief.

In the Moores' kitchen after school, Molly turned up the radio. "Okay, who wants to separate the eggs?" she asked.

"You can do it," said Peichi, who'd just walked in. She was out of breath from walking up the hill to the twins' house.

"I'm not very good at it," protested Molly.

"Then you should practice," Amanda told her.

"Let's both do it, then."

"This doesn't look too hard to do," commented Shawn, peering at the recipe. "I'll melt the butter. I think we should practice poaching the eggs, too." She headed down to the basement to get the supplies. To keep the food for Dish separate from the Moores' supplies, the Chef Girls kept their staples in their very own mini-fridge that they'd bought with the money they'd first made.

"I'll help you," offered Natasha, following Shawn. "So, did you talk to Grandma Ruthie after school?"

Shawn opened the door of the fridge and handed Natasha a carton of eggs. "I tried to, but she was sleeping again. I'll call her later."

Just then, the phone rang upstairs.

"I'll get it!" cried Amanda, even though Molly was closer.

"Go ahead," muttered Molly, rolling her eyes. Amanda rushed over to the phone.

"Hello?"

"Uh, is this Molly?" asked a boy's voice.

"No, it's Amanda." Her cheeks began to flush. Was this Justin? She wasn't sure.

"Hi, it's Connor."

Amanda exhaled. "Oh, hi, Connor. What's up?"

"Uh, is Natasha there?"

"Maybe she is, maybe she isn't." Amanda smirked at Natasha, who'd just come back upstairs, and pointed to the phone. Natasha looked at her, confused, then pointed to herself.

Amanda covered the receiver with her hand.

"It's Connor!" she whispered dramatically.

The girls giggled loudly, saying, "*Oooh, Natasha! Connor's got a crush on you!*"

"*Ssshhh!*" hissed Amanda. "He'll hear us."

"What does he want?" whispered Natasha. She was blushing. "How'd he know I was here?"

Amanda shrugged. "Do you want to talk to him?"

Natasha looked around at her friends. "I don't know! We're still mad at the guys, right?"

Amanda uncovered the receiver and said crisply, "She's *very* busy, Connor. We're all extremely, unbelievably, *incredibly* busy. Call back later when we're not so *busy*. 'Bye!" She quickly hung up the phone.

Laughter exploded in the kitchen.

"That'll show them!" cried Peichi. "For mowing us down on the skating rink!" And the girls began to laugh all over again.

Brrrriiinnnnggg! The phone rang again, and the girls screamed.

"I'll get it! I'll get it!" squealed Amanda. "Hello? *Sssshhh,* you guys, I can't hear!...Oh, hi, Mr. Jordan."

The kitchen went silent.

"...I'm fine...here's Shawn." Amanda quickly handed the phone to Shawn.

"Hi, Dad...she is?...okay...okay. I'll see you in a minute. 'Bye."

Shawn hung up the phone with a sigh. "My dad's

coming to pick me up," she said. "Grandma Ruthie may have to go to the hospital, so he'll have to fly down to South Carolina."

"Are you going to stay with us if he does?" asked Molly.

"Yeah. Dad called your mom at work already. Anyway, he wants me to come home early so we can talk about everything."

That night, as the twins helped each other with math homework, they heard the phone ring.

Mom came into their room. "It's Shawn," she said.

The twins went into the den, each with an extension.

"Hi, Shawn," they said. "How are you?"

"I'm okay. But Sonia called about half an hour ago, and Grandma Ruthie's going into the hospital for sure. Tonight!"

"Oh," breathed the twins.

"Dad said it's because she'll be more comfortable there. But I wonder if she's getting worse, and he's just not telling me. Anyway, he's flying down there tomorrow morning. I told him I wanted to go, too! But he won't let me 'cause I have that big science test on Friday. I'm really bummed that I'm not going with him."

"Of course," said Amanda sympathetically.

"The good thing is that I'll be here for the Dish job on Saturday," added Shawn. "I'll be staying with you guys starting tomorrow. Your mom knows—Dad just talked with her."

"Okay," said Amanda. "We'll help you study for your test."

Shawn sighed. "I just hope she gets better now that she's in the hospital. But—what if she doesn't?"

"Don't think that way, Shawn," Molly said quickly. "She's gonna get better. You have to believe it."

"You've got to, Shawn," said Amanda encouragingly. "Do it for her."

"That's really hard for me to do," said Shawn slowly. "But I'll try."

When the twins hung up, they faced each other, thinking, *What if Grandma Ruthie doesn't get better?*

It was too horrible to say out loud, even to each other.

chapter 5

Before the girls knew it, it was Saturday morning. The Chef Girls had gotten through the week, with their math tests, science tests, music lessons, and after-school activities, but today there was no sleeping in. The girls had been up since seven-thirty to prepare for the big brunch. Though the girls had shopped for the food and made the strawberry butter and a coffee cake the night before, they'd arranged with Ms. Dupree to do most of the cooking at her house. The popovers and eggs Benedict had to be served immediately after they were prepared.

Mrs. Moore drove the girls over to Ms. Dupree's house in her big old Cadillac, the one she'd inherited from her Aunt Hazel.

"Mom, can't you at least *paint* this car?" asked Amanda with a pout, as they loaded boxes into the trunk.

Mrs. Moore laughed. "You mean you don't like gold?"

Amanda wrinkled her nose. "It's not really gold, Mom. It's *trying* to be gold. And the black top is tacky."

"I love my big old gold car with the tacky black top," said Mrs. Moore, her eyes twinkling. "And I'm keeping it until it dies, so you might as well get used to it!"

I'll never get used to this big ugly thing, thought Amanda.

Half an hour later, Mom parked the car in front of Daphne Dupree's home, a beautiful stone townhouse with a turret and a green wooden door.

"Wow," exclaimed everyone, including Mom.

"Look at all those stained-glass windows!" Natasha pointed out.

"I'll bet the kitchen is going to be awesome," commented Molly, opening the car door.

"I think you'll get a nice tip," said Mom with a wink. "Have fun!"

Just then, Ms. Dupree opened the front door. She was petite and very stylish in a pale pink silk skirt, a white blouse, and a wide pink suede belt that was tied at the side. Her short-cropped black hair showed off a pair of lustrous pearl earrings that gleamed against her cocoa-colored skin.

"Hello! *Er*—come in," she said. "The kitchen's straight ahead." She seemed surprised about something, but she smiled politely at each of the Chef Girls as they introduced themselves and went inside.

Wow! What a kitchen, thought the girls. It looked like something out of a decorating magazine. For one thing, it was huge—even bigger than the Moores' kitchen—and uncluttered. Everything was new, from the stove that had two ovens, eight burners, and a big funnel, to the oversized chrome refrigerator. Even the gleaming faucets on the kitchen sink were elegant! The walls were a warm terra cotta color, and the modern cabinets were a tawny beige. It wasn't homey like the Moores' kitchen, but it was beautiful.

As the girls began to put down their boxes of supplies in the kitchen, Ms. Dupree cleared her throat. "Um—I'll be decorating outside in the garden while you're cooking." She patted her professional-grade stove. "Do you have any questions about the stove?"

The girls shook their heads.

"Well, let me know if you have any questions. About anything...anything at all."

"Okay," said Molly.

"Terrific," said Ms. Dupree, though it didn't sound like she meant it. She moved toward the door that led to the garden. Then she turned back sharply and said, "You *have* catered parties before, right?"

"Right!" said Peichi cheerfully. "And they were even bigger than this party!"

The girls stifled giggles.

"All right," breathed Ms. Dupree. "I'll be outside. Remember, this has to be perfect—it's a very special day for my guests and me. Let me know as *soon* as you need help with anything." After gathering up some of the flowers she'd been cutting at the sink, she marched outside.

"Now I'm nervous," whined Amanda. "What if we mess up? She'll freak out on us!"

"Don't worry; we won't mess up," Shawn reassured her. "She probably didn't expect a bunch of kids, that's all."

"Come on!" said Molly to the group. "Let's get started. We'll show Ms. Dupree that Dish rocks!"

"Ohmygosh!" whispered Natasha an hour later as she came back into the kitchen. *"Famous people* are at this party!"

Most of the guests had arrived, and the Chef Girls could hear lots of laughing and talking going on in the garden, which Ms. Dupree had decorated with white netting. She'd set three tables with pink table linens, shining silverware, and center-pieces of fresh-cut flowers. Natasha had gone outside to bring Ms. Dupree the crystal champagne glasses.

"Who's out there?" asked Shawn, who was helping Peichi slide the popover pans into one of the ovens.

"That lady who does the movie reviews on

Entertainment Today!" exclaimed Natasha. "And Maris Miller from *Good Day, America!* She's the one who's getting married."

"Maris Miller?" gasped Molly. "She's one of the most famous TV reporters!"

"Is Ms. Dupree famous?" asked Peichi, but nobody knew.

Things were beginning to feel hectic. While Natasha finished making the fruit salad and putting it in three different bowls, Molly and Amanda carefully made the hollandaise sauce. While they were glad they'd done a practice run, they didn't think it was all that difficult to make.

They combined egg yolks and lemon juice and whisked them together in a saucepan over low heat until it was slightly thickened. Then Molly took the pan off the heat and added melted butter into the pan a little at a time, while Amanda kept whisking it. They added salt, pepper, and some more lemon juice.

Molly tasted the sauce with a spoon. "It's good. Light and lemony."

"And it's such a pretty color of yellow," added Amanda happily. "Okay, time to start poaching the eggs!"

Just then, Ms. Dupree appeared. "How's everything going?" she asked. Her eyes darted around the room.

"Everything's almost ready," Molly assured her. "By the time the popovers come out of the oven in twenty minutes, the eggs Benedict will be ready. Oh, would you please give us some baskets for the popovers?"

"Certainly!" said Ms. Dupree. She reached up into a cupboard and brought out a few baskets and pink cloth napkins to line them with.

"I have to tell you something," Ms. Dupree began, looking around at the girls. "It's just that—you all look so *young* to have your own catering business. I was surprised when I saw you get out of the car. And worried!" She chuckled, showing her pearly teeth. "Er—how old are you, exactly?"

"Shawn and I are twelve," Natasha spoke up. "And everyone else is eleven."

"But Amanda and I will turn twelve next month," Molly said.

Ms. Dupree's eyes grew wide. "Twelve? Eleven?" she gasped. "When I was your age, I could barely break an egg into a bowl! Well, I'm very impressed with you girls!"

"Maybe you shouldn't say that until the food's ready!" joked Peichi.

"I'll leave you alone now," said Ms. Dupree. "Please use the china plates I've set out for you."

It was so helpful that Ms. Dupree had two ovens. Molly and Amanda were able to toast the English muffins in one while the popovers baked in the other.

Once the muffins were toasted, Molly and Peichi

placed each muffin-half on a china plate and laid the pieces of pink smoked salmon on each muffin-half. Amanda carefully placed the eggs in a large pan full of simmering water. She kept them there until they had poached and the whites were set but the yolks were still liquid. Then she lifted them out with a slotted spoon and drained them on a paper towel as Shawn brought out the popovers.

"Whew, I'm glad that part is done," said Amanda.

Peichi quickly helped Shawn take the popovers out of the pans.

"They're so tall!" she exclaimed.

"The strawberry butter's outside already, right?" asked Shawn.

"Right," said Natasha. "One bowl on each table."

All the girls helped put an egg on top of each muffin with salmon. Molly spooned some hollandaise sauce over the eggs, and Amanda garnished them with freshly chopped chives for more color.

"Wow! We did it!" cried Peichi, looking at fifteen china plates. The eggs were covered with the pretty yellow sauce, and the pink salmon peeked out from underneath.

"Let's get these out there," ordered Molly. "I'll bring the coffeepot. *Woo-hoo!* We're done!"

"Molls, don't forget clean-up," Amanda reminded her.

The next day was Sunday. In the afternoon, the Chef Girls and Elizabeth met up at the Brooklyn Public Library to study together. It bordered Prospect Park, a famous park that New Yorkers called "Brooklyn's Backyard." All the girls lived in houses or apartment buildings right near the park.

They loved living in Brooklyn because it seemed to have everything. Prospect Park had a bird-watching center, an ice-skating rink, meadows that went on forever, thick woods, a zoo, and a lake where the girls rode pedal boats in the warm weather. Their extended neighborhood had a world-famous botanical garden and art museum, movie theaters, a puppet theater, funky toy stores, and restaurants serving food from China, Thailand, Japan, Italy, England, Poland, Russia, France, and the Middle East. If this wasn't enough, only a quick subway ride under (or over—depending on which train you took) the East River was the island of Manhattan, otherwise known as "New York City" and "The Big Apple"!

Molly looked up toward a high window, where sunshine was streaming in. "I can't believe we've been here for three hours!" she exclaimed. She stretched her arms and wiggled impatiently in her seat. "I'm finished with my homework. Do you want to go soon?"

"Let's walk down to Harry's," suggested Shawn. "It's only a few blocks away, and we haven't been there in a long time!"

"Good idea!" said Peichi. "Elizabeth, has Natasha taken you to Harry's yet?"

"No, what is it?"

"You'll see," said Amanda. "It's our favorite place to hang out!"

"*Aaahh!*" exclaimed the girls as they walked into Harry's fifteen minutes later, inhaling the smell of brewing coffee. They hated the taste of coffee, but it sure smelled great.

"This place is so cute!" cried Elizabeth, looking around at the polished wooden floor, small marble tables, and mismatched china teacups that decorated the coffeehouse.

"We don't hang out here much," Molly told Elizabeth, "'cause it's expensive. It's an old pharmacy—see the big wooden cabinets? That's where the medicine bottles used to be. *Oooh*, let's grab that table with the armchairs!"

"This is a lot better than a pizza place," observed Elizabeth. "*Hmmm*. What should I get?"

"The brownie," suggested Shawn, getting in line to order.

"No, the lemon bar," said Amanda.

"Yum! I'm getting a strawberry smoothie!" announced Peichi, looking up at a wooden board that listed the specials.

"It's time to call our moms," Molly reminded the friends. While the girls were allowed to walk around Park Terrace without their parents, they had to be with a group and check in often.

As Molly headed toward the back of the coffeehouse to use the phone, a woman got up from a table and began to walk toward her.

It was Daphne Dupree! She gave Molly a big smile.

"Hello!" said Daphne. "Um—"

"Molly," said Molly with a grin.

"Right," said Daphne. "Well, what a coincidence! I was going to call you today!"

"Really?" asked Molly, puzzled. "Did we leave something at your house?"

"No, no. Are you here with your friends?"

"Yes, we're up front."

Daphne turned and signaled to a handsome man at her table that she'd be right back, then followed Molly to the girls' table.

"Hi, Ms. Dupree," chorused the Chef Girls.

"Hello! As I was just telling Molly, I was going to contact you today! You see, I'm a TV producer at *Good Day, America.* Have you ever heard of it?"

The girls giggled.

"Sure," said Natasha. "With Maris Miller and Thacher Hurley. We have it on every morning at our house!"

Ms. Dupree smiled. "Good! Well, I had an idea after

you left yesterday. I want you to be guests on the show for an interview—and do a cooking demonstration!"

The girls gasped.

"You mean, we'd be on TV?" asked Natasha, not believing her ears.

"Absolutely," said Daphne. "We have an open time slot a week from tomorrow. That's a Monday. What do you say?"

"Absolutely!" cried Amanda. She looked around. "Right, everyone? We want to do this!"

"But we'll have to ask our parents," Shawn spoke up.

"Yes, of course," said Daphne. She pulled a pen out of the pocket of her jean jacket. "Why don't you write down your phone numbers, and I'll talk it over with each of your parents. Just think, girls: If they say yes, you'll be seen live—by millions of people all over the country!"

chapter 6

To: mooretimes2; BrooklynNatasha
From: happyface
happyface: Chef Girls! :-@ I can't stop
thinking about the fact that WE ARE GOING
TO BE ON TV! We're going to be famous! My
parents think it's great . . . WHAT ARE ALL
YOUR PARENTS GOING TO TELL DAPHNE DUPREE?????
Especially yours, Natasha? ☺ I'm keeping
my fingers crossed!

BrooklynNatasha: Hi everyone! Guess what,
my parents actually said OK! :-0 And I think
they are as excited as I am! Just think,
here I am on the school paper and now I
will be interviewed by one of the most
famous journalists in the whole world!
That is SO WEIRD!!!!

mooretimes2: Guess what, our parents said
OK too! Our mom was like, "It'll be an
educational experience for you girls." We were
like, "Hel-lo! We're going to be celebrities!"
. . . Hi, it's Shawn now, Dad said OK and that
there will probably be a limo to pick us up,

they do that for these kinds of shows!

BrooklynNatasha: WOW! I guess that's so they don't have to worry you'll be late ☺ My mom wants to come with me . . . I feel like a geek

happyface: Don't, cuz my mom sez she's coming 2!! WOW a limo

mooretimes2: Ours, 2 . . . maybe we'll need 2 limos!!!!!!!

happyface: I want a white one

BrooklynNatasha: I hope the neighbors see me get in the limo!!! GTG, Mom sez 2 much computer time ☹ b-b MWA

happyface: c ya

mooretimes2: 2morrow we'll talk about what we're gonna cook!!!!! Let's meet B4 class in Main Hall. B-b   <3   <3   <3

   "You know, this could be the best thing for our business," commented Molly the next morning when the Chef Girls met up in the crowded Main Hall.

   "We'll never have to put up flyers again," said Shawn with a laugh. "So, what should we make? I wonder if they want us to make a whole meal or just one thing?"

   "A whole meal?" shrieked Peichi. "That's too much."

"I know!" said Molly, snapping her fingers. "Let's make a soufflé!"

"A soufflé! What's that?" asked Peichi.

"It's cool. I just saw a chef make it on one of those cooking shows. You just whip up some eggs and stuff, and bake it in the oven until it puffs up!"

"You mean like a popover?" asked Peichi.

"No, not like that. Anyway, it's really dramatic and French when you bring it out of the oven. It's so...celebrity chef-y!"

The girls began to crack up, but Amanda groaned. "Molls, we never even made a soufflé in *cooking class!*"

"Daphne is probably calling our parents right now!" said Peichi. "You guys, this is going to happen in a *week! Aaaah!* See you at lunch!"

In Amanda, Peichi, and Shawn's English class, the students were writing their personal essays. But Amanda had other things on her mind.

What am I gonna wear to the interview? she thought as she stared down at her blank paper. *The blue velvet poet's top? No, the puffy sleeves will drag in the food...the green-and-black stripey shirt? No, I look like a caterpillar in that...*

Suddenly, a note folded into a triangular

60

shape appeared on her desk. Peichi had coolly dropped it there on her way to the pencil sharpener.

Amanda glanced up to see if Mrs. Weyn was looking in her direction, then slowly unfolded the note. It said:

> I can't concentrate on school!
> We're gonna be on TV! I'm nervous!

Amanda looked up at Peichi, who was slyly looking her way. She smiled and mouthed the words, *Me, too!*

Meanwhile, Natasha was in study hall. She had plenty of studying to do, but instead she brought out a pretty leather-bound book with gilt edging. It didn't look super-girly, so she never worried that people would know she was writing in her diary.

She turned to a clean page and wrote:

I'm so amazed that we're going to be on TV. I'm nervous! I can't believe I'm going to meet Maris Miller! But what if she asks me a question and I open my mouth to talk and all the words come out wrong? What if my hair looks bad that day? What if our food comes out wrong?

Boy has my life changed lately. I'm not as shy as I was before. I have a whole pack of friends. I already have a scrapbook of my articles for the Post. I'm in Dish! And I danced with a boy at my first dance, even though it was just Connor! I wonder what'll happen next? The funny thing is that on my birthday when the fortune-teller came to my party, she said I'd be a TV star seen by millions of people. I can't believe that's going to come true!

Amanda couldn't wait to tell Ms. Barlow about her upcoming TV appearance. She hurried down to the drama classroom right after her last class.

"Ms. Barlow! You're not going to believe this," she said breathlessly. Ms. Barlow was going through scraps of fabric in a big box from the costume department.

"What! What *is* it? Nothing *bad*, I hope?" asked Ms. Barlow, her hazel, lushly mascaraed eyes wider than ever.

"No, it's good! Dish will be on *Good Day, America!*"

Ms. Barlow gasped. "That *is* amazing, Amanda! I don't believe it! How did this come about?"

Amanda told Ms. Barlow all about Daphne Dupree.

"Anyway, Ms. Barlow, you've been on live TV before—"

"Yes, I was a regular on *Weekend Comedy Live!* And it was a fan-*tas*-tic experience."

"What if I get nervous and my words come out all funny?"

"Ah! Here's a great little exercise. Before you go on, say, 'Lips, teeth, tip of the tongue, lips, teeth, tip of the tongue' several times. It'll help your diction. And here's a great breathing exercise. Watch me." Ms. Barlow stood up, then exhaled as she bent over quickly.

Amanda giggled. "You sound like a horse when you do that."

"But it'll keep you focused and relaxed! Now try it with me."

Meanwhile, both Molly and Shawn were outside on the field. Shawn was learning a new cheer, and Molly was pitching at softball practice.

"Strike!" called the coach.

"*Yesss!*" cried Molly. This was the second player she'd struck out—in a row!

Practice ended and everyone walked off the field, dusty and hot. Molly caught up with Athena, the seventh-grader who'd been tutoring Molly all year. It was Athena who'd encouraged Molly to try out for the team.

"Good job, Molly," said Athena. "And you're gonna get even better! Who knew you could throw such a fast ball?"

"Thanks. Hey, listen to this!" Molly told Athena about the upcoming interview.

"Wow!" said Athena. "I can't believe it! Aren't you nervous?"

"Yeah, I'm unbelievably nervous," Molly admitted. "I'm glad I did so well in practice today—it took my mind off the interview!"

Shawn and Elizabeth walked together into the locker room after cheerleading practice. Angie was already in there, getting dressed.

Elizabeth had been Angie's latest victim. Angie had been mean to her for no reason recently—probably because Elizabeth was such an outstanding cheerleader—and Elizabeth now stayed as far from Angie as she could. "See ya, Shawn," she said, feeling grateful that her locker was nowhere near Angie's.

"So, what's up, girlfriend?" asked Angie. She smiled more warmly at Shawn than usual. "I miss you."

"Well," Shawn hesitated. "I'm going to be on TV next week." She told Angie about the cooking job that had led the Chef Girls to meet Daphne Dupree.

Angie snickered. "Dish is going to be on TV? Why? What's so great about Dish? I just don't get it."

Shawn felt like Angie's words had stabbed her.

"What do you mean, what's so great about Dish?"

"Never mind," said Angie. She shrugged and made a funny face. "I was bad. Sorry!"

"See you later," Shawn said coldly, grabbing her back-pack. "I'm walking home with Molly and Elizabeth."

"What-*ever*," said Angie, rolling her eyes. "I *said* I was sorry."

After all that! Shawn's thoughts raced as she walked past girls laughing, talking, slamming locker doors. *After she told me she was sorry about Grandma Ruthie and that she got held back in school, she had to go and say something like that! She's jealous. She can't stand it when she's not the center of attention. She's mean, she steals stuff, I never know what she's gonna do next. I've just about had it with that girl!*

Shawn was pretty quiet as she walked home with Molly and Elizabeth.

"What's wrong?" Molly asked after they dropped Elizabeth off. "Tough practice?"

"Yeah," said Shawn. "Something like that." She really didn't feel like getting into the whole Angie thing with Molly.

"We're home!" Molly called out as soon as she opened the front door.

"Hi," Amanda said, greeting them.

As soon as Molly looked at her sister, she could tell something was wrong.

"Uh, Shawn," Amanda started. "Your dad called."

Shawn gasped. "What is it? Grandma Ruthie? Tell me, Amanda!"

Amanda took her friend by the hand. "Calm down, Shawn. It's not that bad."

"Then what?" Molly wanted to know what was going on, too.

"Your dad just decided that it's probably best if you fly down to be with Grandma Ruthie this week. She's been asking for you. Your dad will call school in the morning to tell them you'll be out. And our dad will take you to the airport after dinner." Amanda gave Shawn a big hug. "Don't worry, Shawn. We're here for you."

"Yeah," added Molly. "Even when other people aren't."

As Shawn sat in the back seat of Mr. Moore's car later that evening, she wondered what Molly had meant by her last comment. Had the twins figured out that things with Angie weren't so great these days?

Later, waiting for the plane to take off, Shawn thought about Angie. She couldn't stay mad when she knew that Angie had confided in her, and trusted her. *I'm going to give Angie another chance,* she decided as she fiddled with her CD player. *That's what a real friend would do.*

he next afternoon, the Chef Girls gathered in the Moores' den with sodas and a big bowl of popcorn, and waited for Daphne Dupree's call.

"The speakerphone still works, right?" asked Molly worriedly. She anxiously pushed buttons.

Everyone excitedly chattered and giggled as Dad's old cuckoo clock ticked its way toward three-fifteen, which was the time Daphne had arranged to call the girls.

Three-fifteen came and went.

"She's late!" Peichi said.

"Well, she's probably really busy," Natasha spoke up. "Having meetings with important people and stuff."

Brrriiinnngg!

The girls squealed.

"*Sssshhhh!*" said Amanda, reaching for the phone.

"Amanda, can't *I* answer the phone just once in my life?" asked Molly.

Brrriiinnngg!

Amanda rolled her eyes and said, "Oh, all right!"

Molly pushed the speakerphone button and said in her "grown-up" voice, "Hello, this is Dish. How may we help you?"

The Chef Girls had to stifle their giggles with pillows. They weren't expecting Molly to crack them up like that.

"Hello, Dish! This is Daphne! Are you ready for your pre-interview?"

"Yes," chorused the girls.

"Terrific. Okay, let's start with the basics! Your names, please, starting with the twins!"

Each girl told Ms. Dupree her full name and age. And Molly filled Daphne in about Shawn.

"How did you all get the idea for Dish?" asked Daphne.

Amanda spoke right up. "Well," she said, "it all started last summer! Molly and I were *bored* out of our minds— and sick of the takeout that our parents had been bringing home so much. I was thinking about the chicken piccata that I'd had at Luigi's restaurant a few days before, and suggested that we make it to surprise our parents! So we found a recipe on the Internet."

That's not how it happened! Molly thought. She shot Amanda "the look."

Amanda paused when she saw Molly's glare.

"*Actually,*" Amanda went on, "I just remembered! It was Molly's idea to make the chicken. *She'd* had the chicken piccata. I actually had the spaghetti and meatballs, that's my favorite—"

"All right. Anyway..." Daphne said, trying to move Amanda along.

"*Anyway,*" said Amanda, "we made a whole dinner for our family that day! And it actually tasted good, and we didn't poison anyone with salmonella or anything!"

Daphne chuckled. "And then what happened?"

"*Well!* Then we saw that cooking classes for kids were happening coincidentally in our very own neighborhood!" said Amanda dramatically.

Molly rolled her eyes.

"...And we thought, 'How absolutely *perfect!*'" Amanda went on.

Why is Amanda suddenly talking like Brenda Barlow? wondered Molly. *Get real!*

"...So we signed up for the classes, and so did Shawn, Peichi, and Natasha, and we learned a lot! But meanwhile, our neighbors, the McElroys, had a fire in their kitchen—"

"Really?" interrupted Daphne. "So, Peichi, what happened then?" It was obvious that Daphne wanted to give someone else a chance to talk.

"Oh!" said Peichi. She sat up straight and said, "The twins' mom said that we should help the McElroys, and make them enough food to eat all week. So that's what we did! It was really fun to help people. We roasted a couple of chickens, and stuff like that. Ms. Dupree? What should we cook on the show?"

"We need to talk about that," Daphne replied. "How about a soufflé?" she suggested.

The girls laughed loudly.

"That's what *I* wanted to make," explained Molly. "But we've never really made one."

"I can see that it's not something you'd make for your jobs," said Daphne. "You're usually cooking ahead, right? Since people usually hire you to cook a few dinners to help them through the week?"

"That's right," Natasha spoke up. "Hi, Ms. Dupree, it's Natasha. We won't have much time on the show, right? So maybe we should make food that's easy—um, that can be made ahead? People watching the show can get ideas if they're going to have a busy week."

"Wow!" said Daphne. "You're thinking like a producer! Natasha, I'm impressed. You just came up with what we call the 'hook' for the segment."

The Chef Girls gave Natasha the thumbs-up sign, and she blushed with pride.

"We could make pesto sauce," suggested Amanda. "That's really fast, and easy to demonstrate."

"Maybe we should roast a chicken," said Peichi. "That's something we do a lot for our clients."

"Since there isn't enough time in the segment to actually cook the food, we'll need two of everything," Daphne pointed out. "There will be the food you begin to prepare on the show, and the finished product that you'll pull out of the oven at the end of the segment. I call it the 'magic of television' scene, where the viewers will get to see the food as it would look coming out of the oven."

"Oh, right," said the girls.

"Why don't you decide what you want to do, knowing that you'll have to cook ahead," suggested Daphne. "Then let me know what food you'll bring, and what supplies you'll need us to buy for you."

"Are you really going to send a limo to pick us up?" asked Peichi.

The girls giggled.

"Of course," said Daphne.

"Yay!" shouted the girls.

"This is going to be fun!" exclaimed Daphne. "Call me tomorrow, and we'll figure out the final details. One more thing, girls: Please don't wear logos or kooky patterns like zebra stripes. They don't work on camera. 'Bye for now. Oh! By the way, *Serena* might be on the show that day. She's in town on a publicity tour. With luck, you'll get to meet her!"

"*Really?* Wow!" cried the girls.

"Morning shows are crazy—you'll see—so I can't promise. But we'll do our best to make it happen. Okay? 'Bye."

"'Bye, Ms. Dupree!" called the girls before they hung up.

They looked around at one another, unbelieving. Then...

"Serena!" screamed the girls. "*Serena!*"

"She's the biggest star around right now!" exclaimed Amanda. "Her new CD just came out, and it's all *over* the radio."

"And she's in that new movie, *New York Wedding*," added Natasha.

"Wow," said Molly. "I can't believe what's happening. Well, anyway, what are we gonna make?"

"I vote for lasagna," said Natasha, "because we can easily make up a pan the day before, for the 'magic of television' scene. And then, of course, we'll make one on the show."

"We'll roast one chicken the night before," stated Molly. "That'll be our 'magic of television' chicken. We'll ask Ms. Dupree to have one bought for us to do on the show."

"How about Texas sheet cake?" asked Peichi. "'Cause it feeds a lot of people, gets better the next day, and Shawn can say it's her Grandma Ruthie's recipe. We'll say hi to her on TV!"

"Perfect!" agreed the girls. They decided on the cake, chicken, pesto sauce, and lasagna.

"I can't wait to tell people that we're gonna meet Serena," said Molly, standing up and stretching.

"Maybe we should just keep quiet about that," suggested Natasha. "'Cause there's a big chance that we won't get to meet her. What if we don't meet her and everyone in school keeps asking us if we did?"

"You're right," said the twins at the same time. Peichi nodded in agreement.

"Oh! I just got a great idea!" said Molly. "I've been

wondering about how Maris Miller is going to remember who's me and who's Amanda—"

"You look different enough," Peichi pointed out.

"But I know what you mean, Molly," said Natasha. "Sometimes when you first meet twins, it's hard to remember which name belongs to which twin."

"Right! So why don't we buy some T-shirts, and get our names printed on the front of them? Each of us will wear one! We'll really look like a team!"

"That's a great idea!" agreed Natasha.

"There are so many of us, it'll definitely help Maris Miller! And there's enough money in the treasury to pay for them," noted Peichi.

"Lulu's Closet has pretty T-shirts," said Amanda. "Let's get those! We're gonna look great!"

Meanwhile, Shawn was following her dad and Sonia into the hospital room. She held her breath. She was afraid she would start crying when she saw Grandma Ruthie lying in a hospital bed.

"Grandma Ruthie," whispered Shawn. "Grandma Ruthie?"

Sonia smiled. "She's still asleep! I guess we'll—"

Grandma Ruthie's eyes opened. "I'm not asleep," she said crossly.

"Yes, you were," teased Sonia.

"No, I wasn't. Hand me my eyeglasses, I can't see a thing."

"Yes, ma'am."

Grandma Ruthie put on her glasses, and then she smiled weakly. Shawn exhaled with relief.

"There you are, Shawn," said Grandma Ruthie. Her voice sounded faint. "I'm just so thrilled that you came down here to see me."

"Oh, Grandma." Shawn leaned down to kiss her grandmother's cheek. "I've missed you." She smiled and reached for her hand. "You don't look sick."

It wasn't really true.

"Don't Sonia and I get a hello?" asked Mr. Jordan, bending over to kiss his mother's forehead.

"Oh, I said hello to ya'all earlier today," said Grandma Ruthie. "That's enough."

O-kay, thought Shawn. *She's really grumpy. That's not like her.*

"Hand me my hairbrush," Grandma Ruthie ordered Mr. Jordan as she slowly sat up. "I can't be looking like a ragamuffin—with my elegant granddaughter here—all the way from New York, can I?" She breathed heavily.

"You won't believe what Shawn did for you today, Mama," Mr. Jordan said, handing her the brush.

"I made you dinner!" exclaimed Shawn. "As soon as I

got here, I made all the stuff you like!" She brought out containers of food that was still warm. "...Corn bread, some nice chicken soup, and buttered beans!"

Grandma Ruthie reached for Shawn. "Come here, baby. I just can't believe it. It all smells so good. You're just growing up so nice."

Dad and Sonia looked at Shawn and smiled.

"I figured you'd be pretty tired of hospital food by now," said Shawn as she put the food on a tray. "Here ya go! *Now* you're gonna feel better."

Grandma Ruthie slowly sat up and tried the soup.

"How is it?" asked Shawn anxiously.

"*Mmm, mmm, mmm.* That *sure* is good. Your mama would be so—proud of—you." Grandma Ruthie leaned back against the pillow.

Shawn's heart sank. Was Grandma Ruthie finished eating already?

"Is that all you're gonna have, Grandma? You haven't tried the corn bread, or the beans."

"I'm just taking a breather, baby. Don't worry, I'm going to eat it all up...I just need to rest a little bit." She leaned back against the pillow and closed her eyes.

To: mooretimes2
From: Ruth Jordan
Re: from Shawn

Hi, M&A. Wuzzup? Deets on pre-interview with DD, pleeezzzzz!

Well, Dad and I am here @ G-ma R's house and it's weird that she's not here. Can u believe she got a cool new notebook, I'm typing on it right now. Guess what I did! I made dinner for her 2day. It was good—chicken soup, buttered beans, and corn bread. Dad and Sonia and I had it for dinner 2. Everyone was impressed.

But G-ma didn't eat much. ☹ She was 2 tired. It made me sad. She's really not getting any better. I'm sleeping in her big bed, it makes me miss her a little bit less.

I miss u guys 2. Thx 4 everything. TTUL. BK—MWA!

Luv,

me

After Shawn sent the e-mail, she folded her arms and stared at the screen.

Angie probably feels really bad now for making fun of Dish, she thought. *Especially since she knows I already feel so bad about Grandma Ruthie. I'll let her know I've forgiven her, and she'll write me right back.*

Shawn began to type.

To: AngieNYC
From: Ruth Jordan
Re: from Shawn in SC

Hi, Angie. I'm here with my Grandma Ruthie. I got here last night. I'm getting used to flying by myself, this is like the 3rd time now! Well, G-ma is not any better. She was really tired 2day. It's really bumming me out!

Wuzzup with you? Is Coach Carson giving you guys a hard time with those roundoffs, ha ha ;-)

E-me when you get a chance.

L8R g8tor

Shawn

Before going to bed, Shawn checked her e-mail. It was very late, and she was exhausted from the stress of the last few days. But her mood brightened when she saw that the twins had replied.

To: Ruth Jordan
From: mooretimes2
Re: for Shawn

Wuzzup back, Chef Girl! Your dinner sounded yumeeeee! Pre-interview went well but Amanda talked too much (sez Molly)!

No I didn't (sez Amanda). :-P

It's Molly again, tomorrow's my game against Bensonhurst. Wish me luck!

We miss u 2. ☹ It was good to have our mega-sleepover last week. We're so sorry to hear that G-ma R isn't getting better. We'll b sending healthy thoughts down to her. Say hi to GR for us.

L8R!

Mwa.

Luv,

us

Other than the e-mail from the twins, Shawn's mailbox was empty.

Angie's online every night, thought Shawn. *I can't believe she didn't write me back. Friends are supposed to be there. Does she care about me or not?*

8

"**M**olly's up!" said Amanda excitedly the next afternoon. She was seated between Peichi and Natasha on the bleachers at the Windsor Middle School ballfield. "Go get 'em, Molls!"

"Go, Molly! You can do it!" called Peichi and Natasha.

Molly didn't look over at the bleachers. She was concentrating on her swing.

"She's a lefty!" called someone on the Bensonhurst team.

The Bensonhurst pitcher rolled her eyes.

"Look!" said Peichi. "She's not used to pitching to a lefty! That's good!"

At the first pitch, Molly swung too soon.

"Strike one!" called the umpire.

The friends stifled groans.

"Don't rush it, Molls! Take your time!" called Amanda encouragingly. "Molly's a better pitcher than a hitter," she muttered to the others.

This time, Molly swung too low.

"Strike *twooo!*"

"Is she golfin'?" joked one of the Bensonhurst players.

Molly ignored the comment and concentrated. *Follow through*, she told herself.

CRACK! Molly hit the third pitch dead center!

"Yesss! Run, Molly!" cried her friends.

Molly made it to second base!

"Woo-hoo!" cried the Windsor team. Molly looked over at her friends and flashed a grin.

"Way to go!" shouted Amanda, and Molly nodded to let her know she'd heard her.

"Molly's really nervous about a big game that's coming up," Amanda told her friends. "Windsor is playing Marine Park. They're Windsor's big-time rivals! And tough. Most of their players are eighth-graders this year."

"You know what would be fun?" asked Peichi. "We should have a party for Molly afterward. In your garden."

"You're right!" said Amanda, nodding. "If Windsor wins, it'll be a victory party."

"What if we lose?" asked Natasha.

"I guess it'll take Molly's mind off of it," said Amanda. "Yes! Molly's at third!"

Just then, a tall girl with wavy black hair got up to bat.

"Oh, good! It's Athena. She's great," Amanda told the girls.

CRACK! Athena hit a line drive. And Molly made it home!

"Yay!" cheered the friends and the Windsor fans that crowded the bleachers.

Flushed and happy, Molly got a pat on the back from Coach Jaffe, then waved at the girls.

"Oh! I just had a great idea!" said Peichi. "For the party, let's make cupcakes, and we'll frost them to look like softballs!"

"Cool!" said the girls.

"Let's make it a surprise!" suggested Peichi.

The others groaned.

"We'll try!" said Amanda.

Molly struck out the next time up at bat.

The game was close, but Windsor beat Bensonhurst, 4-3.

"...At least I didn't strike out every time, like the last game!" Molly told the girls afterward. They'd met her there to walk home together. "I can't wait to e-mail Shawn tonight and tell her that I got a hit. Oh, I hope Grandma Ruthie's feeling better today."

"Yeah," agreed Peichi. "I'm going to write Shawn after dinner—"

"Get *this!*" Nella Zapolsky was saying loudly to a nearby group of girls.

Peichi paused, curious about why Nella was so excited. The Chef Girls turned to see Nella gathering the girls close.

"...Angie Martinez...at her old school," Nella was saying inside the huddle.

"No way!" exclaimed the girls. "*Oooooh!*" They began to giggle.

Nella saw Peichi and the others looking her way. She quickly walked over to them, looked left and right, and whispered dramatically, "You won't be-*lieve* this. Angie Martinez is supposed to be in seventh grade! She got held back a year at her old school!"

"What?" asked Amanda, not sure of what she'd just heard.

"Angie Martinez! The cheerleader! She had to repeat fifth grade at Saint Theresa's!"

The Chef Girls flashed one another a look. What Nella had said made sense. Angie *did* look older than everyone else in the sixth grade.

"Why else do you think she changed schools?" Nella went on in a low voice. "Anyway, I heard it from my cousin Ivy, who's best friends with Julia Carlino, who knew Angie at Saint Theresa's."

Nella darted back over to her friends, who were still giggling.

"Well, even though Angie hasn't been very nice to us," said Peichi, "I know *I* wouldn't want people to talk about *me* like that."

Molly nodded. "It might not even be true. And we've all known since second grade that Nella has a big mouth."

"I'm not going to tell anyone what we just heard," stated Natasha.

"Me neither," agreed Molly.

"Not even Shawn?" asked Amanda.

"Well—" said Molly, hesitating. "No, not even Shawn. Maybe she already knows anyway."

Amanda nodded. One part of her agreed with the others.

But another part of her, the part of her that had been so hurt by Angie's meanness, whispered, *Angie's just getting what she deserves with this gossip. I could finally get her back by telling her that I know all about it.*

Then Mom's voice came into her mind: *Treat others the way you want to be treated.*

"Let's go," said Amanda, picking up her backpack. "Ready, Molls?" Suddenly, she wanted to be anywhere but there with all that buzz.

Amanda didn't like the way she was feeling. She didn't want to be like Nella Zapolsky. She wanted to be like Peichi and Natasha and Molly and Mom.

But why did that suddenly seem so hard to do?

That night, the twins wrote Shawn an e-mail telling her about the game. They didn't mention the rumor about Angie. They kept their message light, since Shawn had sent another sad e-mail saying that Grandma Ruthie seemed even worse than yesterday.

Things looked bad.

"Maybe she's going to die," Molly told Amanda as they sat together, re-reading Shawn's message.

"Don't say that."

Molly sighed. "Oh, she's got to pull through. She's got to."

The girls went upstairs to bed, but both had trouble sleeping that night. Both were worrying about Grandma Ruthie—and Shawn.

"Amanda! I'm glad you're early. I've got some news," said Ms. Barlow the next afternoon. She seemed rather tense.

"Hi, Ms. Barlow. What's the news?"

"*Well.* Sophie Wexler has mononucleosis!"

"What? Sophie's *sick?*"

"Yes, she's out for a month! Don't worry, darling, she's not going to *die*. She just needs *lots* of rest, poor thing. But as for *me*—I have to replace her for this *very* important role! And guess who I'd like to replace her with?"

"You mean—me?"

Ms. Barlow nodded enthusiastically.

"You want *me* to play the part of Miss Claudia Crumb?" Amanda shrieked happily. *"Really?"*

"Yes! I think you'd do just *fine* in it! What do you say?"

"Absolutely!" Amanda exclaimed. "Thank you so much! I can't wait to get started!"

That night at dinner, Amanda told her family the big news.

"That's wonderful, Manda!" said Mom.

"Ms. Barlow believes in you," said Dad. "She sees that you have talent."

"Very *raw* talent," teased Molly.

"That's no way to talk to the sister who's throwing you a party," said Amanda. Then she clapped her hands over her mouth. She'd just given away the secret!

"Huh?" asked Molly.

"So it's not a surprise?" asked Mom, looking relieved.

"Not anymore," said Amanda, wincing.

"A party? For me? Why?" asked Molly, looking around at everyone.

"For your big game against Marine Park," said Amanda. "It's not a big deal; we'll just have hot dogs and cupcakes and stuff. Okay?"

"Cool," said Molly. She smiled at Amanda. "Thanks!"

After dinner, the twins went upstairs to check their e-mail. They were surprised to see that Shawn still hadn't written. Amanda asked Mom if she and Molly should call Shawn.

"Not tonight, sweetie," replied Mom. "Her family's going through a tense time. I'll call Shawn's dad in the morning, though, and I'll pass on your good wishes."

"Okay," agreed Amanda. "Well, I guess I'll go send out the invitation to Molly's party now." She headed back to the den and began to type, even though her heart felt too heavy to concentrate on a party.

After rehearsal the next day, Amanda hurried to her locker to get her books. Rehearsal hadn't gone very well. Amanda felt overwhelmed by how many new lines she had to learn—and the play was only one month away!

She saw Angie up ahead, leaning against the lockers with Sara Schneider and Monica Timboli, two tough eighth-graders who wore a lot of makeup. They'd been chewing gum and talking loudly, but they suddenly got very quiet when Amanda arrived at her locker.

Amanda's heart started pounding as the girls began to whisper and giggle. She grabbed her books as quickly as she could, not even taking the time to put them into her backpack. She closed the door, hooked on the lock, and turned to go.

Had the girls moved closer to her?

Suddenly, they seemed to be right in her face.

Amanda tried to smile as if nothing were wrong, but as she tried to walk, her left shoe didn't move right away. It was stuck to the floor.

With a huge wad of pink gum.

"Oh, would ya look at that," said Angie, pointing. "Whatta shame. Ha ha!"

She rolled her eyes as if to say, *Loser!*

Amanda began to shake. Suddenly, everything seemed to be happening in slow motion with the sound off.

Don't cry, don't cry, Amanda told herself. *What am I gonna do how am I gonna get out of here I can't walk all the way down the hall with gum sticking to me...*

Something made her look up. The girls were now casually walking away, as if they'd done nothing at all.

You're not getting away with this, Angie, thought Amanda. *Not this time.*

Amanda threw her backpack to the floor—SLAM!—to make the girls turn around.

It worked.

"At least *I* didn't get held back a year at school, *Angie*," Amanda heard herself saying. It was as if someone else was speaking through her, making her lips move. Her voice didn't even sound like her own.

Then she was shouting, her voice echoing down the long hallway. "We know all about it, Angie! It's not a *secret!*"

chapter 9

"*Ohmygosh!*" cried Molly in the twins' bedroom when Amanda got home. "*Ohmygosh,* Amanda! I can't believe you said that! I can't believe she did that!"

"I know," said Amanda, shaking her head.

"*Then* what happened?"

"She just turned and kept walking, Molly. That was it. The other girls gave her a weird look, like, *Is that true about you?* I got out of there *fast.* And then I ran all the way home!"

"So—how do you feel now? Are you glad you said it?"

Amanda looked down at the floor. "You know, when I fantasized about saying something like that to her before, I thought it would feel good. But now that I've really said it, it doesn't feel good at all. Mom would be so bummed at me. Don't tell her."

"I won't," Molly assured her. "Gee. I hope Angie doesn't do anything to get you back."

"Me, too," said Amanda, shrugging. "What can she do?"

The twins were silent. But both were thinking, *Angie could do plenty.*

"Come on, let's check our e-mail," Molly told Amanda. "It's Friday night. Let's forget about Angie."

To: mooretimes2
From: Ruth Jordan
Re: from Shawn

Sorry I didn't write yesterday but G-ma R got worse. She went on oxygen. That means she can't breathe on her own. You guys, the doctor told us that she might die. I cried so much after I walked out of her room. I'm supposed 2 come back tomorrow nite but I'm scared to leave her. I don't want to miss GDA with u guys. But what if she gets even worse after I leave? I know u don't have the answers but anyway write me back. Plus would u guys be mad @ me if I wasn't there for GDA?

TTUL

Shawn

The twins wrote back right away.

To: Ruth Jordan
From: mooretimes2
Re: for Shawn

Hi Shawn,

We're so sorry about everything.

You should do whatever you think is the best thing. Being on TV 2gether is cool, but it's not the biggest deal in the whole world. Your family is more important than us being on TV. So of course we wouldn't B mad @ you! If you do come back, though, at least G-ma R will be able 2 see you on TV! And you know she'd get a mega kick out of that.

Mwa!

M&A

Shawn wrote back a few minutes later.

To: mooretimes2
From: Ruth Jordan
Re: from Shawn

Hi. Thanx for writing. Well Dad said that he is staying here past Saturday, but I HAVE 2 come back on 2morrow b/c I'm gonna get behind in school, and he doesn't want me to miss out on being on GDA. He sez there's not much for me 2 do around here except B depressed any-way. So I'll be back 4 sure 2morrow

(flying alone AGAIN, how BORING and
DEPRESSING). I'm just really hoping
that G-ma R will pull thru. Dad sez
she's 2 tuff not to, but he looks
really worried. And I don't know what
2 believe since grownups are always
lying 2 kids 2 protect them from stuff,
which is dumb.

    xoxox

    Shawn

PS So anyway that means I'll be staying
with you guys again when I get back.
Dad is calling your mom about airport
stuff.

Shawn hit SEND, then checked her e-mail. Once again,
her mailbox was empty. Angie had never bothered to
answer Shawn's e-mail!

So much for Angie, thought Shawn sadly. *I was even
willing to give her another chance.*

On Saturday night, the twins went with Dad to pick up
Shawn at the airport.

"How's Grandma Ruthie?" Molly and Amanda asked,
giving Shawn a hug.

Shawn looked tired, but she smiled. "I have some good news. She's better now. Just since this morning. She might be going off the oxygen soon. They say it'll take a little while, but she'll improve."

"Oh, good," said Dad and the twins. They were relieved to see Shawn smiling.

"Thanks for picking me up, Mr. Moore," said Shawn, as Dad placed her suitcase in the trunk of the car.

"It's not a problem, Shawn," said Dad with a grin. "You're like family!"

Shawn shyly looked down at the ground and smiled. "Thanks."

The girls talked nonstop all the way home, and drove Dad crazy flipping the radio station every time a song came on they didn't like.

"...so anyway, that's how I got the bigger part in the play." Amanda had breathlessly told Shawn all about the latest developments.

"You'll love the T-shirts we got at Lulu's Closet for the show," Molly told Shawn. "We had our names put on them at the mall. They look so great!"

"Oh! I promised I'd make the Texas sheet cake for the show," said Shawn suddenly, as Dad pulled up to the house.

"So we'll make it together, tomorrow," said Amanda. "No big."

"But you don't have a jelly roll pan," said Shawn with a big sigh. "We'll have to go to my house and get one. Does

Good Day, America have the other one we'll need? Did anyone think to ask Ms. Dupree that?"

"We did tell her," Molly assured Shawn. "We gave her a complete list of the food, seasonings, and equipment we'll need for the demonstration. And we're bringing the cake, a baked pan of lasagna, and a roasted chicken that they'll warm up for us, to take out of the oven for the 'magic of television' part...Are you okay?"

Shawn sighed. "I'm panicking. I didn't write my history paper, and I barely studied for the science test on Tuesday. I couldn't concentrate, you know? I have so much to do tomorrow, and then the show's the morning after that! I'm really getting nervous about being on TV."

"But at least with you, it won't show," chuckled Molly. "You're the cool, calm, collected type, remember?"

As if, thought Shawn.

Later that night, the girls were hanging out in the twins' room, painting each other's toenails. The house was quiet because everyone else was asleep. Shawn had curled up in her bed, the one that folds out of the twins' big armchair.

"So, Shawn, there is a little more news that we didn't tell you in the car," began Amanda, who was perched on the window seat, holding her old stuffed giraffe.

"What else? You got a bigger part in the play, Molly got a hit, and you all had the pre-interview. How'd I miss so much in less than a week?" joked Shawn.

"This is big," said Molly. "Amanda had a run-in with Angie, and—and, well, did you know that—" She looked at Amanda, not sure what to say next.

"Know what?" asked Shawn, sitting up in the bed.

"Did you know that Angie was held back a year?"

Shawn didn't answer right away. She finally asked, "How did you know that?"

"So you *did* know."

"Uh-huh, Angie told me. Who told *you?*"

"Nella Zapolsky was spreading it around the locker room."

"Oh, boy," said Shawn with a heavy sigh. "I hope Angie doesn't think *I* told you. I promised I wouldn't tell anybody, and I haven't."

Molly shrugged. "Well, it's not like getting held back a year is, you know, a *tragedy*. It happens sometimes. Plus, when you're all grown up, it won't matter anyway."

"I know," said Shawn. "I wonder how Nella found out?"

"From someone at Saint Theresa's, Angie's old school," replied Amanda. "This is what happened. I was about to leave school after rehearsal, and I ran into Angie and those two tough eighth-graders she hangs out with. And..."

Even though Shawn was tired from a difficult week, she had a hard time sleeping after hearing Amanda's story. *I just know Angie's gonna blame me,* she thought. *Oh, well, if she does, I'll just set her straight, that's all. No big. I guess. I hope...*

chapter 10

Molly could feel the bright lights in the TV studio on her face as Maris Miller asked her questions. She told Ms. Miller all kinds of things about Dish, and Kitty, and Mr. Flint's homeroom...

Then she heard a loud beeping sound over and over, which drowned out Maris's voice.

Sorry, I couldn't hear you, Ms. Miller. Ms. Miller? Uh, Maris?

"Molly, honey. Wake up. It's four-thirty."

Molly opened her eyes to see Mom in her bathrobe, not Maris Miller. Mom's long arm reached over Molly to turn off the beeping alarm clock on the nightstand. A light streamed out from the twins' bathroom, where Amanda was already washing her face. Shawn was sitting up, rubbing her eyes.

It was Monday morning.

"Oh. Oh." Molly sat upright in bed, her heart beginning to pound. She quickly swung her legs out from under the blankets. "Did I oversleep?"

"No, sweetie," said Mom, stroking Molly's hair. "Everything's fine, and all the food you made yesterday is ready to go, remember?"

Molly stood up. "Oh," she said, relieved.

"All you need to do is get ready," Mom said gently.

"Okay."

It was *very* early in the morning!

"Amanda, what are you doing?" asked Molly, dressed in her new jeans and the shirt. "Mom wants you downstairs now. She wants you to eat something."

"I'm just using the curling iron a little. My hair looks flat! So does yours, let me fix it—"

"Amanda, the limo's gonna be here any second and they're picking us up first and we can't make everyone late! Put that thing down and *come on!*"

"The limo's here," announced Dad ten minutes later. He'd been watching for it at a window. "Girls! Barbara!"

Down the hall in the kitchen, the girls shrieked.

"Let's go!" said Mom. Carrying the chicken and the pan of lasagna, the twins hurried out the door, kissing Mr. Moore quickly on the way out. Mrs. Moore rushed in and out a few times. Shawn came out last, carrying the cake. For a moment, the girls stood still when they saw the shiny black limo waiting for them.

"Bye, girls," said Dad in a low voice so that he wouldn't wake the neighbors. "Have fun! Matthew and I will be watching! And Poppy! And Grandma Ruthie and your dad, Shawn!"

One by one, everyone came out of their front doors and got in the limo: first, Mrs. Cheng and Peichi, who waved eagerly, and then Natasha and Mrs. Ross.

"Isn't this *exciting?*" giggled Mrs. Ross. "I haven't ridden in a limo in a long time! Or been to a television studio, ever!" She patted the leather seat with her manicured hand.

Shawn and the twins stared at her. They'd never seen her so—enthusiastic. Mrs. Cheng and Mrs. Moore giggled then, too.

"You're as excited as we are, aren't you?" Molly asked the moms.

"Sweetie, this is a big deal!" exclaimed Mrs. Moore. She leaned over to Mrs. Cheng and Mrs. Ross, and said, "We'll be in the greenroom with all the guests on today's show. I wonder who we'll get to meet?" The three women began to chat excitedly.

But as the limo glided over the Brooklyn Bridge and toward the towers of midtown Manhattan, the Chef Girls became quiet. They were deep in their thoughts, preparing for one of the biggest days of their lives.

Finally, the limo pulled up to CSM Studios, where news headlines flashed electronically around the front and side of the building.

"Look! We're right in the middle of Times Square," said Peichi, who was the last one to get out of the car.

"Wow," said Molly as everyone looked up in awe at the skyscrapers and office buildings around them. "I didn't know it was all lit up so early in the morning!"

"The flashing signs are almost as big as some of the buildings they're on," said Natasha. "I love that. And look, there's the top of the Empire State Building!"

"And there's the *New York Times* building," Mrs. Ross pointed out, "with the old clock on top! That's what Times Square is named for, you know."

"There's Broadway," said Amanda, looking across the street. "Look at the theaters all in a row. I wanna go to every one of these Broadway shows!"

Just then a CSM Studios security guard greeted the group, checked his clipboard for their names, and said to the moms, "You'll need to wear these." He handed them each a sticker that said VISITOR and the date. He placed a quick phone call, and a few minutes later, a young woman with short brown hair came to greet everyone.

"Hi, I'm Pam, a production assistant for the show. I'll take you up to the greenroom."

She led the group to what looked like a living room, where the guests sat on comfortable sofas and watched the show as they awaited their turn to go on.

"Hello, girls!" said Daphne, walking quickly toward them. She looked amazing, with a pale yellow silk sweater and a cream-colored skirt. With her was a young man with short red hair and a friendly smile. Daphne introduced herself to the moms, and said, "Please make yourselves comfortable, ladies. There's plenty of coffee." She led them to a table with coffee urns, a colorful basket of fruit, and a large plate of doughnuts and bagels.

Then Daphne turned to the girls. "Now, girls, you're off to the makeup room. Then you'll be brought back here to wait until it's time for your segment. This is my assistant, Todd. He'll take the food you brought and will give it to the food stylist. She'll make sure that the food is put in the oven at the right time. Okay?"

Everything's moving so fast now, thought Molly.

Here we go, thought Amanda. *I can't believe this is happening!*

The girls waved good-bye to their beaming moms and followed Daphne, who walked quickly down a hall that had framed photos of famous TV stars and newspeople.

"Um, Ms. Dupree? Do you think we'll get to meet Serena?" asked Peichi.

"I hope so, but I just can't promise it," replied Daphne over her shoulder. "Her agent confirmed that she'll be here, but we're scheduled so tightly. She's staying at the hotel across the street, and probably won't get upstairs until after you've left." She led the girls into a small, comfortable room that had a mirror with lightbulbs all around it. "This is Stephano, our fabulous makeup artist. Okay, girls, see you in a bit!" And Daphne was off, her high heels clicking.

The girls forgot their disappointment about Serena when Stephano greeted them. He had gelled, spiky black hair, emerald green eyes, and a goatee. He was so handsome that all the girls blushed when he asked their names.

"I thought the makeup artist was going to be a woman," Peichi murmured to Amanda.

"Actually," said Stephano, who'd overheard Peichi, "there are lots of male makeup artists. Have a seat! You get to go first!"

Peichi giggled, embarrassed that Stephano had heard her. As she climbed into the chair, she asked, "Are you gonna make up Serena?"

"No," said Stephano with a wry smile. "She brings her own makeup artist wherever she goes. Too bad for me! But," continued Stephano as he began to brush some powder on Peichi's face, "this very brush touched Gwen Alfani's face yesterday!"

"Gwen Alfani!" shrieked Peichi. "She's one of my favorite singers! I'll never wash my face again!"

The girls began to chatter as Stephano joked and laughed with them.

As Amanda got into the chair, she said, "Stephano, I'm gonna need some extra makeup."

"Why?" asked Stephano, as he searched for the right shade of powder for Amanda's pale skin tone.

"I have circles under my eyes this morning; can't you see them?"

Stephano chuckled and shook his head. "You girls have beautiful, perfect young skin. All you need to look absolutely gorgeous is just a little powder and lip gloss...maybe a hint of blush. But the grownups? Oh, *boy* do they need a lot of help!"

"Like, what do you do for them?" Molly wanted to know.

"I can make their acne disappear! I can make their noses look thinner or their eyes set wider apart! It's amazing what you can do with makeup."

As Stephano worked, Amanda began to do one of the breathing exercises that Ms. Barlow had taught her. Molly rolled her eyes in embarrassment, and the other girls giggled.

"Don't laugh," said Amanda. "This helps you relax. Right, Stephano?"

"Exactly," said Stephano, trying to hide a smile. "Gwen Alfani did it, too."

By the time Todd ushered the girls back to the green-room, they'd begun to feel tense. There was nothing to do now but wait.

"Who's that man?" Amanda asked. The moms were shaking hands with a friendly looking white-haired man wearing a blue suit. They were very impressed with him.

"That's Jimmy Carter!" said Todd. "As in, former president Jimmy Carter."

"Really?" asked Peichi. "He was the president?"

Todd chuckled when he saw the girls' blank looks. "I guess you're too young to remember him. He recently won the Nobel Peace Prize. It's a big deal that he's here! Anyway, you're on in about fifteen minutes..."

Fifteen minutes! Yipes! thought all the girls.

"...Eric, the stage manager, will come in to get you when it's time," added Todd. He handed each girl a chef's apron. "Here are your aprons! You can take them with you afterward. Daphne wants you to put them on now."

"Oooh!" cried the girls. Each girl had gotten one in a different color.

"They're pretty, but...so much for the T-shirts with our names on them!" groaned Peichi after Todd rushed off. "What a waste of money from the treasury!"

"Why is she making us wear aprons for the interview?" Amanda wondered aloud.

She got her answer just then, as a lanky young man approached the girls.

"Hello, girls, I'm Ben, the audio guy. I'm here to set you up for sound so that all your fans at home can hear you! Okay, let's do this quickly, one at a time." Starting with Peichi, he held a tiny microphone close to the top of each girl's apron, letting the wire run down the back of the apron.

"I see, the apron will hide the wire," said Amanda.

"Right. This way, we won't have to run the wire down your shirts," said Ben as he carefully tucked the wire around the top of Peichi's pants to hide it. He then clipped the audio pack to the back of her pants.

"This is called a 'vampire clip,'" said Ben, pointing to the microphone's clip that had little teeth on it. He clipped the microphone underneath the front of the apron. "Now please reach in underneath and pull down that wire so it hangs straight. Thanks! Now I need an audio check to check your levels. Can you count to ten, please?"

"One, two, three, four, five, six—" said Peichi shyly.

"You're a quiet one," Ben told her.

"Not really!" cracked Molly, and the girls giggled.

"You'll need to speak up," Ben went on.

"Seven, eight, nine, ten!" said Peichi a little louder.

"Good. Thank you. Okay, the audio's good to go," said Ben. He looked at Amanda. "You're next!"

When the girls were ready, Mrs. Cheng waved them over.

"Girls, this is President Jimmy Carter! Mr. President, I'd

like you to meet my daughter Peichi. And please meet Amanda, Natasha, Molly, and Shawn."

"Hello, girls," said President Carter. He smiled and said, "I hear you have your own cooking business!"

"Hello, sir," said the girls politely. They saw the looks that the moms were shooting them that meant, THIS IS A BIG DEAL, GIRLS!

President Carter chuckled and said, "I know you would rather have met Serena today."

The girls smiled. They didn't know what to say.

"When were you the president?" Peichi wanted to know. "And what are you talking about on the show?" Everyone smiled at Peichi's boldness.

"I was president from Nineteen Seventy-Seven until Nineteen Eighty-One," replied Mr. Carter. "I'm here to talk about my work for peace. Have a good show, girls!"

"Thank you," said the girls in unison. The moms nodded ever so slightly at the girls, which was a signal that they could go sit down.

As the girls walked away, Mrs. Moore turned to President Carter and said in a low voice, "Would you be so kind as to sign some autographs for the girls? I know they'll wish later that they'd thought to ask you. Especially since they'll read about you in their history books!"

"Places," said Eric the stage manager, striding into the greenroom. He wore a headset and mouthpiece under a battered baseball cap. "One minute."

Everyone gasped.

"This is it!" said Mrs. Moore. "Good luck, girls!"

The moms reached out to hug the girls, but there was no time.

"Come with me," said Eric, leading them out to two red sofas on the brightly lit set, which looked so...unreal. The lights were so bright, the girls felt as if they were outside in sunlight.

Ohmygosh! thought Natasha as her eyes adjusted to the light. *There's Patti Huang at the anchor desk, ready to report the news! And Bill Shue, the weather guy! I guess that's the screen where the weather map comes up on...and there are the chairs where Maris Miller and Thacher Hurley do their interviews every morning—but it looks so different with all the cameras!*

Everything looks so different than it does on TV, thought Shawn. *It's not cozy at all.*

The room didn't look so inviting in real life because it was open and there were camera and sound crews busily working around its edges.

And there were Maris Miller and Thacher Hurley, co-hosts of *Good Day, America!* They were seated together on a dark blue sofa on another part of the set, chatting about something the girls couldn't hear.

It's so weird to see famous people in real life, thought Peichi. *They're...well, real. But they look kind of fake 'cause they're wearing a lot of pancake makeup—even Thacher Hurley and the weather guy!*

"Lips, teeth, tip of the tongue, lips, teeth, tip of the tongue, lips, teeth, tip of the tongue!" said Amanda.

I have to go to the bathroom, thought Molly.

"Thirty seconds!" announced Eric. He went and stood near the camera that was pointed right at the girls.

The girls swallowed hard as Maris Miller came toward them. She was wearing a pretty pale-green spring suit, and her short blonde hair gleamed under the lights.

"Hello, girls!" she said warmly. "Welcome to the show! Ready? Here we go!" She sat down in a red chair facing the girls and watched Eric for her cue.

"Stand by! Camera, three, two—" said Eric, who also signaled the numbers with his fingers—then pointed his index finger at the camera. A red light on the camera signaled that it was on.

"We have some very interesting young guests today," said Maris Miller into the camera. "Their names are Peichi Cheng, Shawn Jordan, Molly and Amanda Moore, and Natasha Ross. They call themselves the Chef Girls! They're from just across the river in Park Terrace, Brooklyn, and— I know from *personal* experience that they're quite the gourmet cooks. They even have their own business, called Dish! That wouldn't be so unusual, but these girls are just eleven and twelve years old! Good morning, girls; thanks for coming."

"Good morning, Ms. Miller," said Molly. She was sitting up as straight as she could.

"Good morning," said the rest of the girls.

Score! thought Molly. *I was the first one to answer, and I remembered to say 'Ms. Miller!'*

"Molly Moore, I'd like to start with you," said Maris Miller. But she was looking at Amanda.

Amanda opened her mouth to say something, but Molly spoke up first.

"*I'm* Molly, actually," she said with a little laugh.

"Oh, I'm sorry. I know that you and Amanda are twins. I can't keep your names straight! Anyway, Molly, what gave you the idea for Dish?"

Ms. Miller was so warm, so friendly, that Molly began to relax. She smiled and said, "Well, Amanda and I had fun cooking dinner for our family one day. Then all of us signed up for a cooking class. Um, then one day, our neighbors had a fire in their kitchen? So we cooked a week's worth of dinners for them, to help them out. That's kind of how it started." Molly knew her face had become bright red, but she was grateful that she hadn't stumbled over her words as she usually did when she was nervous.

"I see!" said Ms. Miller, her blue eyes sparkling. She looked at Peichi. "Peichi, what do you like best about having your own business?"

Peichi's eyes grew wide, and she opened her mouth to speak—but no words came out.

"Uh—" she gulped.

Peichi was speechless!

Natasha jumped in while Peichi composed herself. "We like knowing that we're helping people," she said. "For instance, sometimes we cook for free, as we did for the neighbors who had the fire, or if someone is new to the neighborhood, or having a baby."

"How do you find the time?" Ms. Miller asked as she looked at all the girls.

Amanda was just about to answer the question when Ms. Miller looked down at the notes on her lap and said, "Peichi, you take flute and Chinese lessons. Amanda, you act in school plays. Shawn, you're a cheerleader, and Natasha, you write for the school paper. How do you girls manage to have a business, too?" She looked up at Shawn.

Hey, you forgot my softball and piano! thought Molly.

Shawn smiled. "It can be hard to find the time to do it all," she admitted. "And once, when almost all of us got the flu at the same time, we had to hire some of our friends from cooking class—plus our cooking teacher—to help out on a big job!"

Ms. Miller laughed. "That's great. Now, what sorts of things do you cook on a typical job?" She looked around at all the girls.

Amanda was just about to reply, but Natasha spoke

up quickly and said, "Usually a client wants dinner for several nights. So we have to make food that can easily be reheated, that will stretch for a few days. We'll often roast a chicken, or make lasagna, or a pasta sauce...sometimes all three!"

Ms. Miller looked over at Peichi kindly, a sign that she was encouraging her to talk.

"Whuh—"

Peichi felt her throat close up, so she just nodded and smiled brightly.

"...And we always make a homemade dessert!" Amanda added perkily. Ms. Miller laughed appreciatively. "Wonderful!" she said, and quipped, "Do you deliver to Manhattan, where I live?"

"We don't drive yet," replied Amanda, smiling at Ms. Miller's little joke. *Whew,* she thought, *I got something in—and it was even funny!*

Ms. Miller looked at the camera and said, "We're going to take a short break, and then the Chef Girls are going to cook for us! We'll be right back."

"You have two minutes," Eric told Ms. Miller and the girls, "to get to the kitchen set, put on your chef's hats, and be ready to go."

"Okay, girls, let's go!" said Ms. Miller. As the group

hurried over to the gleaming white-and-steel kitchen set, Ms. Miller said, "You girls did a wonderful job on my bridal shower. Thank you! I really loved those popovers, by the way!"

"She's so nice!" Natasha whispered to Amanda. "And look at this kitchen! Cool, huh!"

"It's almost as fancy as Ms. Dupree's," giggled Amanda.

Ms. Dupree and Todd were waiting for the girls.

"Here are your chef's hats," said Ms. Dupree as Todd handed one to each girl. "What are they really called? I know there's a French word."

"*Toques,*" replied Natasha. "Oh, look! They say *Good Day, America* on them!"

"Daphne, you think of everything!" exclaimed Ms. Miller as Todd helped the girls put them on. "That's such a nice touch. The girls look great!"

The Chef Girls blushed at all the attention.

"And you can keep them," Daphne told the girls. "Now, is everyone settled? Does everyone know what they're going to talk to Maris about here?"

The girls nodded.

"Remember, girls, look into the cameras with a nice smile as Maris does your introduction, so that the viewers can see your faces," Ms. Dupree reminded them. "Since there's more than one camera, always look into the camera with the bright red light."

Meanwhile, the oven was on, with the lasagna and the

other chicken warming up inside. The cake
that Shawn had baked yesterday was sitting off
to the side, waiting to be shown off at the end.

"Camera, three, two—"said Eric, pointing to the camera.

"I'm back with the Chef Girls!" said Ms. Miller enthusiastically as the girls drew in near her and smiled into the camera. Ms. Miller draped her arms over Amanda's and Natasha's shoulders and said, "Natasha, you're making lasagna. That's a good choice because you can make it ahead, right?"

"Right!" said Natasha, as she placed another layer of noodles on the cheese. For some reason, she wasn't nervous at all! "And you can freeze it, too. We're using a homemade sauce here, but you don't have to. There are lots of good bottled sauces out there, and it saves time. But you know, it's nice to make a homemade sauce on a Sunday when you have time."

"It sure is," said Ms. Miller. "You're a real chef, Natasha! Now, Amanda, what are you doing with this chicken?"

"I'm rubbing a mixture of olive oil and herbs under the skin."

"That'll lock in the flavor. Can I try?" asked Ms. Miller.

"Sure," said Amanda. "Just do it like this."

"...And Molly and Peichi are looking *very* professional as they prepare to make pesto sauce," Ms. Miller went on. "Peichi, is pesto something you make often for Dish?"

Peichi froze. She'd been crushing a garlic clove with a

large knife. Suddenly, she feared that she would cut herself in front of millions of people if she used the knife while talking.

She stopped and nodded slowly, looking blankly into the camera. Then she saw Daphne, off to the side, pointing to Ms. Miller.

Whoops! Look at Ms. Miller! she told herself, so she quickly did, still nodding.

But Molly had jumped in. "Pesto is so easy, you just make it in the blender," she told Ms. Miller as she expertly tore some big stems off the basil leaves.

CRASH!

Molly's audio pack had just fallen off and clattered to the floor. Startled, Molly shifted and felt her foot crush a pointy thing—Ms. Miller's shoe!

Whoops! Molly thought. *I'm such a dork!* She looked up apologetically at Ms. Miller.

"That's true, it is easy," noted Ms. Miller, not missing a beat but with her eyes twinkling at Molly as if to say, *Don't worry about it!* "It's so good on pasta," she added. "Shawn, what are you making?"

"Texas sheet cake. Whoops! I just dropped an egg."

"There it goes," said Ms. Miller, looking under the table. "Crack!"

Shawn knew Ms. Dupree would want her to just keep going, so she just smiled and stirred the chocolate mixture on the stove. "Anyway, this feeds a lot of people, so it's good for Dish, and picnics or parties. It's my Grandma Ruthie's recipe, so it's special to me."

"And she's not feeling so well these days, right?"

"That's right. She's in the hospital, so we'd all like to say—"

"Hi, Grandma Ruthie!" cried all the girls and Ms. Miller, waving at the camera.

Grandma Ruthie clapped her hands over her mouth and said, "Oh, I just can't believe it. Did you hear my little baby doll!" She waved back at the TV in her room, then turned and grinned at Sonia and Jamal—who couldn't believe their little Shawn was on TV like it was no big deal!

"Aha! Thacher is coming over," said Ms. Miller. "I knew you couldn't resist, Thacher."

"This lasagna looks perfectly done," declared Mr. Hurley as Natasha proudly brought the pan out of the oven. "I can't wait to try some! Good job, Natasha."

"*Mmmm!*" said Ms. Miller, taking a bite of the cake. "This is delicious! And look at that gorgeous chicken. Thanks, Chef Girls! Now over to you, Bill, for today's weather!"

Eric smiled at all the girls and said, "Great job, girls! I'm gonna rush you back to the greenroom. Quickly, quickly..."

Wow, is that it? wondered Molly.

I barely remember what I said, thought Natasha.

I hope I didn't say anything stupid, fretted Shawn.

All that work and now it's over already? thought Amanda.

Wait! I didn't get to say anything yet! thought Peichi.

Maris and Thacher waved good-bye to the girls, saying, "Thanks again, girls!"

"Oh! You were terrific!" chorused the moms when the girls arrived.

"Yay, it's over!" said Peichi as she hugged Mrs. Cheng. "It was fun, except when I couldn't talk!"

"I never thought I'd see *that* happen," Mrs. Cheng teased her.

Just then, Ms. Dupree rushed into the greenroom, followed by Ben.

"Congratulations, girls! It went so well!" she exclaimed. "You're some of the best guests we've ever had on the show! Gotta run. Ben's here to help you remove those audio packs. Congratulations, girls, and thanks again! I'll call you the next time I need some cooking help!"

Natasha watched Ms. Dupree hurry off. She longed to

say something to her...*Being on this show taught me so much. Now I know for sure what I want to be when I grow up.*

But it was too late. Ms. Dupree was out the door.

Then the most amazing thing happened. Ms. Dupree had dropped a little piece of paper. It fluttered to the floor as she disappeared down the hall.

"Be right back!" Natasha told the group, and rushed over to the note. She quickly picked it up and caught up to Ms. Dupree.

"Ms. Dupree, you dropped this!" called Natasha.

Ms. Dupree turned around. "Oh, thanks!"

"Um, it was so cool to be here today," Natasha began, her face reddening. "To see how things are done on TV, and to see all that goes into one segment. And to meet Maris Miller!"

"I'm glad you got so much out of it, Natasha," said Ms. Dupree happily. "You were wonderful on camera. So relaxed and sure of yourself!"

"I want to be a television journalist someday." There. Natasha had said it.

Ms. Dupree nodded. "When you're in college, maybe you can work here as a summer intern and get some experience."

"What's an intern?"

"An intern works here during the summer, usually for free, to gain experience."

"But that's still a long way away," said Natasha wistfully.

Daphne cocked her head and gazed at Natasha. "Tell you what. I'll bring you here for Bring a Child to Work Day. That's not too far off. I'll show you the entire studio, and you can meet everyone from the camera crew to the news anchors, attend meetings, and see how an entire show is produced!" She unclipped a pen from a pad of paper. "Write your name and phone number here, quickly please—and Todd will call you to set it up!"

"Thank you so much, Ms. Dupree! This has been the most amazing day of my life!"

Natasha practically flew back to the greenroom.

"I'm coming back here on Bring a Child to Work Day!" she announced.

"Wow!" said the girls.

Mrs. Ross beamed at Natasha. "You've become such a go-getter, Natasha! I'm so proud."

I'm proud, too, thought Natasha happily. *For speaking up!*

"Uh-oh!" said Peichi suddenly, looking around the greenroom. "Where's my backpack?"

"I don't have it," said Mrs. Cheng. "Did you leave it in the makeup room?"

Peichi exhaled. "Oh, right."

Just then, Pam walked by. "Excuse me, Pam?" said Mrs. Cheng. "Would you please take my daughter to the makeup room? She left her bag there."

"Sure," said Pam. Then she smiled and winked at the girls. "Why don't all of you girls come? Ladies, they'll meet you in the lobby."

"See you downstairs," said Mrs. Cheng. The women picked up their purses and headed for the elevator.

The girls looked at one another. Did Pam have something up her sleeve? Like a *Serena* thing?

"I'm glad we got to say good-bye to that cute Stephano," giggled Peichi a few minutes later as the girls followed Pam out of the makeup room.

"I wish we could say hello to Serena!" hinted Molly,

looking up at Pam. "Maybe she's down here right now!"

Pam smiled knowingly. "This might be your lucky day! Let's see."

"Really?" cried the girls. They began to whisper excitedly among themselves.

The group turned a corner, and then another, where they came upon a burly man standing near a door.

Pam slowed down. "That's Serena's bodyguard," she said in a low voice. "Why don't you ask him if he'll let you in to meet her?"

The girls stopped short.

"Can't *you* ask him?" Peichi whispered.

"You may have better luck if you ask him," said Pam encouragingly. "How can he turn down a kid?"

"Come on! Let's do it!" urged Molly. She and Peichi hurried down the hall together, giggling, toward the bodyguard.

He didn't look very friendly, but that didn't stop Peichi and Molly. "Can we meet Serena?" they asked. "Please?"

"She's busy," said the bodyguard. "Sorry."

You sure don't look sorry, thought Molly.

"It's okay," said Peichi, trying to sound casual. "We were just on the show."

That just about cracked everybody up!

Just then, a young woman's voice called out from the dressing room, "Oh, let them come in, Bobby."

It was Serena's voice!

The girls tried to stifle their shrieks as the big body-guard smiled in spite of himself and let them in.

Molly led the way. At first, all she saw was a big TV with President Carter on, talking to Thacher Hurley. Then she saw in the mirror a reflection of a woman with long, dark, curly hair. She turned around. There was the real Serena, smiling at her!

"It's the Chef Girls!" said Serena as the girls filed in. "Hi! I just saw your segment. You did so well! Did you save me a piece of that Texas sheet cake?"

The girls gasped. Serena was seated in front of her personal makeup artist, a young blond guy. Serena wore a pink-and-white striped velour sweatsuit, and her feet were bare. Her nails were painted a glimmery, pale lavender. She looked smaller in real life. Even without makeup, she was prettier in real life, too.

That was when Amanda began to cry. "Oh," she said, "sorry. This is too much!"

Everyone laughed.

"Tell me your names," said Serena. "This is Ken, by the way."

"Oh, you made me goof," clucked Ken as he lost Serena from his grasp. "Stop moving around, Serena."

"I'm Peichi!" said Peichi, waving.

"Hi, I'm Molly."

"And I'm Amanda!"

"Hi, Serena, I'm Shawn."

"And I'm Natasha."

"It's nice to meet you all. I just got up, so I'm a little sleepy," said Serena. "So, you have your own cooking business! Do any of you want to grow up to be chefs?"

Molly smiled and motioned toward Amanda. "We want to have our own restaurant someday."

"That's a great idea!" said Serena. "I own a restaurant here in New York. I love to cook, myself. What's your favorite thing to make?"

Here the girls were with one of the biggest stars ever, and she was interested in *them!*

Amanda was the first to recover from being starstruck. "Dessert," she quipped. Serena threw back her head and laughed. Even her laughter sounded musical.

"I love dessert, too! And candy. I make candy for my nephews and nieces."

"Come back, Serena," scolded Ken. He checked his watch. "We don't have much time, you know."

"Joanne," Serena called to a young woman across the room, "don't we still have a few freebies lying around?"

The girls turned to look at Joanne, who was sitting in the corner with long hair, dyed black. Unlike Serena, she was wearing lots of makeup, including deep-crimson lipstick.

"I'm on it," replied Joanne with a grin. She began to root around in a big tote bag.

"Are you Serena's assistant?" asked Peichi.

"I'm actually her publicist!" Joanne pulled a big box out of the bag. "How would you girls like Serena's brand-new CD and some signed photos? Now where'd I put that permanent marker? Here you go, Serena."

As Serena quickly signed the stuff for the girls, Pam—who'd been waiting near the door—cleared her throat and said, "Time to go, girls."

"Thank you so much, Serena!" cried the girls. "Bye!"

"Bye!" said Serena, standing up to hug each girl. "Take care and good luck with Dish!"

"*Ohmygosh!*" all the girls chattered as Pam led them to the lobby. "Can you *even* believe it!"

"She even hugged us!"

"She's so pretty!"

"She's so nice!"

As the girls approached their moms, Mrs. Moore said, "Hi! We were beginning to wonder what happened to you!"

"You won't *believe* it, Mom!" cried Molly.

"This has been the most amazing day of our lives!" Amanda chimed in.

The girls told the moms all about meeting Serena.

Mrs. Moore looked at Mrs. Ross and Mrs. Cheng, who were just as surprised as she was. "What a day! I think we should do something special."

Mrs. Ross nodded. "Let's all go out for breakfast," she suggested. "I know a great little place right near Rockefeller Center!"

Natasha couldn't believe this was her mom speaking. "Really, Mom?" she asked.

"We don't have to go right to school?" asked Peichi, looking hopefully at her mom.

"A day like today doesn't happen often," said Mrs. Cheng. "Come on, let's celebrate! New York City, make way for the famous Chef Girls!"

Later, in the limo on the way back to Brooklyn, everyone was still hyped up.

"I can't believe I stepped on Maris Miller's toe!" exclaimed Molly. "I felt like such a geek."

"And I can't believe I dropped an egg on the floor!" groaned Shawn.

"That was funny," said Peichi. "At least Maris made a joke out of it!"

"Natasha, you were so comfortable on camera," said Mrs. Moore. "Who knew you could talk so much? You're always so quiet at our house!"

Molly gasped. "Natasha! Remember at your birthday party, what the fortune-teller said? That you'd be a TV star? Well, you were!"

"Wow!" exclaimed the girls.

"Meanwhile, I'm the actress and hardly said a word," groaned Amanda.

"No—*I* hardly said a word, remember?" chuckled Peichi.

"Oh! I almost forgot," said Natasha, reaching into her bag. "Look, it's a card that Elizabeth made to wish us luck. Pass it around."

"She's really nice," said Molly.

Natasha nodded happily. "Yeah, she's great."

"Do you think she'd like to be in Dish?" asked Peichi.

"I was going to bring that up to you," Natasha replied, looking around at her friends. "Should we ask her?"

"Sure," said Shawn quickly. She'd worried that Elizabeth didn't like her as much since Angie had been mean to her.

"Sure!" agreed the other girls.

"She'd be a real help while I'm in China," said Peichi. "Oh, that sounded so la-de-da, like I go there every day!" She giggled at herself and said in a mock grown-up voice, "I'm so *glamorous!* First I'm on TV, and then I'm off to *China!*"

"Back to reality!" said Mrs. Moore when the limo pulled up near the school.

"Cool!" cried Molly. "The kids in the classrooms on this side of the building are gonna see us pull up! We're celebrity chefs!"

The girls took one last look at their fancy limousine and waved good-bye to their moms before heading inside. They came in just as the bell rang to change classes.

"Wow!" said Molly. "Perfect timing! Everyone's looking at us! And *waving!*"

"Hey, can I have your autograph?" asked a boy.

"Good job, Chef Girls!" called some girl.

Shawn looked at the friends. "What's going on? It's like the whole school saw us or something."

"Hello, television stars," called Miss Hinkle, the school secretary.

"How did this get around?" asked Amanda. "It's not like we told the whole school."

"But someone did," said Peichi. "I wonder who?"

By lunchtime, the girls knew.

In Molly's math class, Justin made a point of standing near the door to greet her as she walked in.

"Hey, Justin."

"Is that any way to greet your publicity guy?" asked Justin with a grin.

"What?"

"Connor and Omar and I found out from Elizabeth that you were going to be on TV. So we told Miss Hinkle, and then the principal made an announcement this morning and said that whoever wanted to come to the cafeteria to see you on TV could come! He had a big-screen TV brought down, and like a million kids came to watch!"

"Really?" said Molly, surprised. "That was nice of you." She smiled at him for the first time since the ice-skating incident.

"So," said Justin with a grin, "you and the rest of the Chef Girls can stop ignoring us now."

"We'll think about it," teased Molly, "after our ice-skating bruises are gone."

"Sorry about that—" Justin began, but he was interrupted by Miss Spontak asking him to sit down.

When Shawn opened her locker that morning, a folded-up piece of notebook paper fell out.

Shawn opened the note and read:

Shawn—
    I can't believe I trusted you. I should have known you'd blab to THE ENTIRE SCHOOL that I was held back a year. How could you do that to me? Watch out. I'm on to you.
        Angie

"I knew it!" Shawn said out loud. She crumpled up the note and looked up at the ceiling. *I knew she'd think it was me. Why couldn't today have just been a perfect day?* She thought about the day ahead. *Luckily, there's no cheerleading practice today...but what am I gonna do at lunchtime? Angie will be waiting for me in the caf.*

Lunchtime came quickly, but by then Shawn had made a decision. She wasn't going to worry about Angie. After what she'd just been through with Grandma Ruthie, the Angie thing didn't seem that important. Grandma Ruthie was alive and getting better, and that was what Shawn wanted to focus on—not petty girl stuff.

As tempting as it was to show the twins Angie's note, Shawn decided against it. *Why ruin everyone else's perfect day?* she decided.

"We're still famous," giggled Peichi as the Chef Girls walked into the cafeteria together. Kids greeted them as they had that morning.

Shawn couldn't help looking for Angie while she waited in line. As the friends chatted happily, Shawn's eyes roved the large room, searching for Angie's hair color. Her ears listened for the shrill voice. But Angie wasn't there.

As Shawn was reaching for a bowl of butterscotch pudding, she heard Jamie Tafoya say, "Shawn?" Jamie was a seventh-grade cheerleader.

Shawn turned around. "Hi, Jamie."

"Great job today, Shawn! I didn't know about Dish. That's cool. Hey, Angie told me to tell you to meet her in the bathroom."

"Which one?"

"The one just down from the cafeteria." Jamie shrugged. "She's in there right now, but I don't know what she wants. Anyway, see you later."

"See you later," Shawn said automatically, but she was picturing Angie leaning against the tiled wall in the bathroom.

Waiting for her.

Oh, so what, thought Shawn as she walked toward the Chef Girls' usual table. *She can rot in there...no, wait. I'm gonna get this over with so I can get on with my life!*

"You guys, I'll be right back, Shawn told her friends. "Um, I need to wash my hands."

She hurried to the bathroom. She saw Angie's reflection as she walked in. She was leaning against the wall, with her hands on her hips. No one else happened to be in there.

"Hello, Angie."

"So, what do you have to say for yourself? You're gonna pay, Shawn. How could you—humiliate me?"

"It wasn't me. Believe me, Angie. I wouldn't do something like that."

"Who else could it have been? I know people are talking about me. It didn't help that Amanda yelled it down the hall—"

"Hold it. I did *not* tell anyone. Amanda heard it from somebody in the locker room. You know, people at this school know people from your old school. Stuff like that just...gets around. I had nothing to do with it." Shawn snapped at Angie.

"Yeah, right," Angie sneered.

"Why do you have such an attitude all the time?"

Shawn shot back at her. "No wonder people gossip about you. You treat Amanda so badly, and now Elizabeth, too. And you didn't even care about how sick my grandmother was. I didn't hear from you at all while I was in South Carolina! You haven't been nice to *anyone!*"

For a moment, neither girl said anything. When Shawn looked back at Angie, she was surprised to see that Angie had tears in her eyes. *Whoa,* Shawn thought. *Maybe I went too far. What do I do now?*

Just then, Angie spoke. "How—how is your grandmother?"

"She's doing better," Shawn answered.

"Good," Angie said softly. She cleared her throat. "Um, sorry I flipped out. I just figured you *had* to be the one spreading the rumor."

Shawn shook her head. "I wouldn't do that to you, Angie."

Angie smiled at Shawn. "I know. Are we cool, girlfriend?" She reached out and put her arm around Shawn's shoulders.

"Sure," Shawn replied. But even though the fight was over, she still felt uncomfortable around Angie.

"I'm glad our moment of fame is over," Amanda told Peichi later that day. "Now we can start thinking about other stuff, like our video."

"And the party for Molly," Peichi reminded her. "Her big game is on Saturday, right? You know, I think we should invite Justin and Omar and Connor. Don't you?"

"I was thinking the same thing," Amanda said. "I'll send an e-vite tonight. Well, I'm off to rehearsal." She gave Peichi a little wave. "I don't know how I'm gonna stay awake. I feel like I've been up for days."

Peichi groaned. "I know what you mean. I was so nervous about this morning that I didn't sleep at all. And now I have my flute lesson!"

The red light on the Moores' answering machine was already flashing rapidly—indicating messages from lots of people who wanted to hire the Chef Girls!

After dinner, Dad pushed the machine's PLAY button for the family and Shawn. "This is a funny one," he said. "Listen."

"Hello? Dish? Hi, this is Lorraine! You girls were just so cute on TV today! And I could really use your help! I've got a full-time job as a secretary at Brooklyn Sewer Rooter Service, and five kids—"

As the girls and Matthew shrieked with laughter, Dad pressed the FORWARD button.

Beep!

"Hello? I'm calling for, um, the Chef Girls? My name's

Mary Mendel? Do you have a cookbook? I'd love to get that lasagna recipe—"

Dad hit the STOP button. "We may have to hire a manager for Dish," he joked.

Later that night, even though all of the Chef Girls were exhausted by their big day, they all resisted falling asleep. There was so much to relive, remember, and smile about in the dark. Peichi had kept her parents up late telling them every detail of the day. Natasha had kept her parents and Elizabeth up late, too—then spent an hour writing about it in her diary.

In the twins' room, Amanda murmured, "You guys?"

"*Hmmm?*"

"This day was so special."

"I know," Molly agreed. "But it felt more like a dream than for real. That makes me kind of sad, ya know?"

"I can't believe it's all over," remarked Shawn sleepily. "The best part for me was knowing that Grandma Ruthie got such a thrill out of it."

"Yeah," said Amanda with a sigh. "I'll never, ever forget being in the TV studio, talking to Maris Miller. And then meeting Serena."

"I still can't believe it happened at *all*," Molly said drowsily. "Who knew that last summer, when we were cooking for the first time, it would lead to us being on *Good Day, America?* 'Night, you guys."

"'Night, Molly."

As the rest of the week flew by, the Chef Girls enjoyed the attention they got from students and teachers. They watched the tapes of their segment that their parents had made, over and over. And they returned all the Dish phone calls, saying that they'd be ready to take jobs again in a few weeks. Things still seemed so hectic for most of the girls.

They'd also invited Elizabeth to join Dish, and although she was so happy to have been asked, she said she'd have to think about it. "I don't know if I really love to cook," she admitted.

Amanda and Peichi shot the audition video in one afternoon. It took a couple of tries, but Amanda finally performed her material in a way she was happy with. Then she and Peichi had fun editing it over the next few days.

Molly and her teammates psyched themselves up for the big game. After being on TV, Molly felt like she could handle anything!

Shawn and Elizabeth cheered at the boys' basketball game and worked hard at cheerleading practice. Angie was quiet in practice. Shawn was pleasant to her, but she didn't go out of her way to be near her.

The Chef Girls spent Friday night preparing for Molly's party. They bought everything they needed at Choice Foods and had fun decorating the "softball cupcakes."

Saturday morning was sunny and hot. It was the middle of May, and summer wouldn't be far behind now.

As the Moores, Natasha, and Peichi arrived at the ball field, Amanda spotted Justin right away. He was sitting alone in the first row of the bleachers, loading his camera. He photographed lots of Windsor games for the *Post*.

"Let's sit there," she suggested to her family and the Chef Girls, pointing in Justin's direction.

"Gee, I wonder why," teased Matthew in a singsong voice.

Amanda decided to ignore him. And she made sure to sit next to Justin.

"Hi, Justin!" she said. "Are you coming to the party today?"

"Hi, everyone," said Justin with a wave. He looked at Amanda. "I'll be there," he said. "Connor and Omar are coming, too."

"Good. Shouldn't you be taking pictures down on the field? Why are you in the bleachers?"

"Oh, I'll head down in a bit, when Athena's up. She's a powerful hitter, and that'll make a good shot."

Sitting next to Justin, it was hard for Amanda to focus

on the game. She chatted on and on with him about the play, and her audition video. "So Peichi did a great job," she was saying. "And I think I have a good chance—"

"Go, Molly!" called Justin suddenly. Amanda blushed with embarrassment. She realized she hadn't been paying attention to Molly.

Crack! On Molly's first swing, she hit the ball hard and straight.

"Run, Molly!" cried Justin, standing up. *"Safe! Yessss!"*

Justin was cheering even louder than the Moores!

But Windsor got only a few hits after Molly was at bat. And it didn't take long to see that Marine Park was the better team. They beat Windsor by six runs.

"That's okay, Molls," said Dad as the family met Molly afterward. "You did a great job striking out that big girl. And you're swing's getting better."

"Is Athena coming over?" asked Mom.

"Uh-huh," said Molly, looking over at Athena, who was being consoled by her parents, cousins, aunts, uncles, and both sets of grandparents. "Come on, let's go. I could use a hot dog and half a dozen cupcakes!"

Molly couldn't help but cheer up as everyone came streaming into the garden for the party. Athena finally showed up, and after a while she was laughing and joking with everyone, the game forgotten for now.

"Good job, Molly," said Justin, putting two of Mr. Moore's grilled hot dogs on a paper plate. "I'm glad I got to see you play."

"Thanks."

Just then, Amanda and Peichi came over.

"So, I heard you guys made an audition tape?" Justin said to Peichi.

"Yeah! It looks great! I did some cool editing stuff with it, too," Peichi exclaimed.

"Do you want to see it?" asked Amanda, brightening.

Justin shrugged. "Sure."

Later, after most people had gone home, Amanda and Peichi played the tape for Justin.

"It looks good," he said. "Peichi did some nice closeups. And, uh, your acting looks pretty good."

"Thanks, Justin!" said Amanda, her face reddening. "Are you going to come to the play?"

"Yeah," said Justin. "Actually, I'll be photographing your dress rehearsal for the *Post*. Well, see ya. I have to take off. I'm going back out to say good-bye to everyone."

"Okay, byeee!" said Peichi.

"See you later, Justin," said Amanda. She sighed. That Justin. He was always running off.

The following Monday after rehearsal, Amanda handed Ms. Barlow her tape.

"Thanks for encouraging me to make this, Ms. Barlow. Do you want to see it?"

"Of course! Let's look at it right now!"

Ms. Barlow didn't say much while she watched Amanda's performances, but she kept nodding her head. When the tape was over, she looked at Amanda and said, "Nice job. It's ready to send in."

"Really?"

"Yes. And you look good on camera. I'll send it today!"

"How long until I find out if I made it?"

"Oh, darling, it'll be a *while*. I'd say at *least* a month. The camp directors will have to review all the tapes and make their decisions, and send out the letters. In the meantime, young lady, you've got a play to prepare for!"

Amanda worked very hard on her role as Miss Claudia Crumb. She practiced her lines over and over, in her best British accent. Sometimes she even dreamed them.

She practiced walking, standing, and sweeping elegantly into a room, the way Miss Crumb was supposed to. She learned how to make her voice carry in the big auditorium. And she slowly realized that this sort of physical training would help her be confident in real life, all her life.

Best of all, she was having a blast! She was doing what she'd only dreamed about before this school year. For three whole nights, the audience would be watching *her!*

And Amanda loved being involved in a project with lots of people. The cast and crew were always laughing together at inside jokes during rehearsal. The eighth-graders were nice to the sixth-graders. The cast would say their lines to each other as they passed each other in the halls.

Meanwhile, the costume crew was putting together some fun and glamorous looks for the girls. After wearing black work boots and a shawl and being covered with soot in *My Fair Lady*, Amanda was so thrilled that she got to be pretty this time that she tried on her costume as often as she could. It was a pink "flapper" dress that had spaghetti straps and hung straight, ending with fringe on the bottom. She got to wear long, long ropes of pearls, a thin rhinestone tiara across her forehead, and delicate little shoes.

And the set began to come together. It was a formal room of a 1920s English mansion, with giant "wooden" bookcases, elegant "antique" furniture (that Ms. Barlow had found at the Salvation Army), and even a spiral staircase.

Suddenly, it was the week of the show, then the night of dress rehearsal. It was also the week of the twins' twelfth birthday, and the Moores had planned to take the twins, their friends, and Poppy, their grandpa, out for a big dinner after the Friday night performance. Saturday night would be the cast party at Ms. Barlow's house.

The cast helped each other with their hair and makeup.

"Wow! You look great, Amanda!" said a few people.

And when Amanda saw herself in the mirror with her costume on, with her deep red lipstick and rouged cheeks, her hair arranged in an elegant style, she thought, *Hey! I do look great!*

Dress rehearsal was like a dream—in some ways, like a bad dream. People forgot their lines. Tiffany tripped on her pointy shoes and stumbled onstage (which made everybody laugh, including Tiffany). At one point, Amanda accidentally said Tessa's line instead of her own because Justin was there taking photos, making her nervous.

"I'm not worried!" said Ms. Barlow when it was over. "A bad dress rehearsal means a great opening night! Go home, get your beauty sleep, and I'll see you tomorrow. Call is at six o'clock sharp!"

Everyone grabbed hands and cheered.

"Now, remember, Mom, *please* don't sit front and center," Amanda said as Mom drove her to the school the following night. "I'll get too nervous if the first thing I see is all of you in a row, smiling at me!"

138

"Okay," promised Mom. "Break a leg!"

Hanging out in the greenroom with the other actors was so much fun. Everyone was hyper—joking, saying their lines to the mirror, putting on makeup, warming up their voices. Bottles of water were everywhere, as were good-luck cards that the cast had made one another. Ms. Barlow dashed in and out, looking like a movie star in her red silk Capri pants and black velvet top.

And finally Sam Wong, the stage manager, said, "Places!"

Amanda's part started late in the first act. *Here goes,* she thought, as the Act One players filed quietly down the hall and went backstage. For some reason, she wasn't nervous. She felt electric, more alive than she ever had before, right down to her fingertips!

And when her cue came, she stood tall and entered the set gracefully.

"...Why, Lord and Lady Ashleigh!" she heard herself saying in a British accent. "How *wonderful* to see you again! How *have* you been?"

Yesss! thought Amanda as Carl Hastings spoke his line to her. *First line down—and it was good!* Suddenly, she was aware of her feet, in those delicate shoes, rooted to the stage floor.

This was where she wanted to be. She never wanted this play, this night, this feeling, to end.

The next week, Amanda felt a letdown. The costumes were put away, and the set was dismantled. The cast missed hanging out with one another. All that work, all that anticipation—and now it was over. And soon school would be over, too.

Amanda spent lots of time wondering if she had made it into Spotlight. During the school day, when she looked up at the clock and realized that Elaine, the mail carrier, had probably been to the house, she pictured a letter waiting for her on the floor in the hallway. That's where the mail fell every day after Elaine put it in the slot on the front door.

But every day, when the twins got home, Mom shook her head and said, "No, sweetie, nothing yet."

Then one day, Amanda and Molly did a favor for Mrs. Tortelli and walked her beagle, Casey. Casey had nipped Amanda on the ankle, which he'd never done. It didn't really hurt, but for once Amanda wasn't thinking about the mail when she got home.

Matthew rushed down the hallway to greet them. He was holding a white envelope and acting more hyper than usual.

Amanda gasped. "What's that?"

"Special *de-liv-ery*, Amanda," said Matthew in his annoying singsong voice. "Here's something you've been *wait-ing* for! Something—"

"Let me see!" cried Amanda, reaching for the envelope.

"Come get it!" cried Matthew, running with the letter up the stairs.

"Give me that, you little shrimp! Come back here!"

Amanda easily tackled Matthew and grabbed the letter. Then she hurried into the twins' room and sat down on her bed, her hands trembling.

As Matthew and Molly stood in the doorway, Amanda opened the letter and read:

Spotlight Arts Camp

May 30, 2003

Dear Miss Moore:

Thank you for sending us your audition videotape, which we have reviewed with interest.

Despite its merits, we regret that we are not able to offer you a place in Spotlight Arts Camp this year.

Thank you again for auditioning for Spotlight Arts Camp, and we invite you to audition again next year. Enjoy your summer.

Sincerely,
Spotlight Arts Camp Staff

"What does it say?" asked Molly.

"You don't look like you got a good letter," said Matthew.

Amanda set the letter aside, not answering right away.

Oh, good, thought Molly. *She didn't get in. We'll be together all summer like always.*

"No," said Amanda, hiding her face in her hands.

Suddenly, all Molly wanted was for Amanda to have gotten in.

"But you'll still have a good summer, Manda," said Matthew softly. "We'll all go to the shore together and see Poppy, and hang out on the boardwalk and ride the rides." He shrugged and gave her his goofy smile. "It would be really weird if you weren't here. What am I gonna do with just *her* around?" He jerked his thumb at Molly.

Amanda giggled and wiped away a tear. Then she let out a big sigh. "Gee, Matthew, I never knew ya cared." She stood up, as tall as she could. "Well, who wants to go get an Italian ice? I'm putting this letter away. School isn't out yet, but my summer's starting right *now.* Come on, let's go!"

"Yeah, let's go!" cheered Matthew.

Molly smiled at her twin. "It's still good that you tried out, right, Manda? Anyway, we've got an unforgettable summer waiting for us. I can feel it!"

Amanda nodded happily. "You're right. I can feel it, too. This summer's gonna be *big.*"

The Amazing cookbook

By

The CHEF Girls

AMANDA!

Molly!

Peichi ☺

shawn!

Natasha!

Peichi's Cupcakes

These were so cute. We made our cupcakes look like softballs, but you can use different colors to make yours look like tennis balls, basketballs, or soccer balls!

makes about 30 cupcakes

Yellow Cupcakes

2 3/4 cups flour

2 1/2 teaspoons baking powder

1/2 teaspoon salt

1/2 cup unsalted butter, softened

1 3/4 cup sugar

1 1/2 teaspoons vanilla

2 large eggs

1 1/4 cups milk

Preheat the oven to 375 degrees.

1. Fill muffin tins with cupcake liners.

2. In a large bowl, blend the flour, baking powder, and salt. Set aside.

3. Using a mixer, cream (beat) the butter and vanilla. Add the sugar gradually, and cream it until light and fluffy.

4. Add one egg and beat well (for about a minute or so), then add the other egg and repeat.

5. Add about a quarter of the flour mixture and mix well. Then

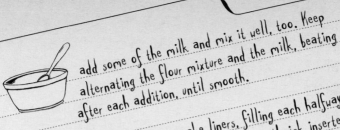

add some of the milk and mix it well, too. Keep alternating the flour mixture and the milk, beating after each addition, until smooth.

6. Pour the batter into the cupcake liners, filling each halfway, and bake for about 15 minutes or until a toothpick inserted into the middle of a cupcake comes out clean.

7. Let the cupcakes sit and cool for 5 to 10 minutes before taking them out of the tins and putting them on the racks to cool completely before icing.

Icing

1/2 cup butter, softened
4 cups powdered sugar
1/2 teaspoon salt
1/3 cup milk

1 teaspoon vanilla extract
white food coloring
1 tube of decorating icing
with small tip

1. Using a mixer, cream the butter until smooth.
2. Add the sugar, salt, milk, and vanilla. Mix until creamy.
3. Add the food coloring. Mix well.
4. Frost the cupcakes.
5. Using the decorating icing, draw little dotted lines on the cupcakes that look like the seams on a softball.

Mom's pasta
all'amatriciana

Mom says there are other ways to make this dish,
but, in my opinion, this way is the best!

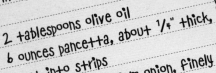

2 tablespoons olive oil

6 ounces pancetta, about ¼" thick,
   cut into strips

1 medium onion, finely chopped

1 large pinch of hot red pepper flakes
   (about ½ teaspoon), or to taste

2½–3 cups canned diced tomatoes
   (with the juice)

salt

1 pound pasta (Mom uses bucatini or spaghetti,
   or even larger penne in a pinch)

⅓ cup Pecorino cheese, grated

1. Bring a large pot of water to a boil with
   1½ teaspoons salt

2. Heat the olive oil in a large skillet over
   medium heat. Add the pancetta and cook,
   stirring occasionally, until crisp and golden brown.
   Using a slotted spoon, take it out of the pan

and put it on a plate lined with a paper towel. If you have a lot of fat left in the pan, you can take some out, but leave about 2 tablespoons.

3. Add the chopped onion to the skillet. Sauté until soft, for about 5 minutes or so.

4. Now stir in the red pepper flakes. Cook for 30 seconds, then stir in the tomatoes and a little salt to taste.

5. Now put the pasta in the boiling water.

6. Simmer the tomato sauce until it thickens—about 10 minutes.

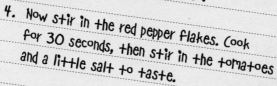

7. When the pasta is al dente (cooked but still firm), drain it and then put it back in the now-empty pot. Add the pancetta and the sauce to the pot, and combine. Add the cheese, toss it again, then serve it to your fans! Yum!

—Molly

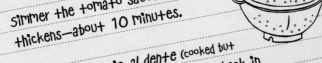

EGGS BENEDICT

IF YOU MAKE THIS, PEOPLE WILL BE IMPRESSED!!

SERVES 4 PEOPLE.

1 TABLESPOON VINEGAR

8 SLICES OF CANADIAN BACON (WE SUBSTITUTED

SMOKED SALMON)

4 ENGLISH MUFFINS, SPLIT

8 EGGS

1 CUP HOLLANDAISE SAUCE

1. MAKE THE HOLLANDAISE SAUCE FIRST AND KEEP IT WARM BY NESTING THE BOWL IN ANOTHER BOWL FILLED WITH HOT, BUT NOT BOILING, WATER. YOU CAN KEEP IT WARM THIS WAY FOR ABOUT HALF AN HOUR.

2. NOW PUT 2-3 INCHES OF WATER, AND THE VINEGAR, IN A SHALLOW PAN. BRING TO A BOIL. THEN LOWER THE HEAT SO THAT THE WATER BARELY BUBBLES.

3. IF YOU ARE USING CANADIAN BACON, FRY OR GRILL THE BACON UNTIL IT IS LIGHTLY BROWNED.

4. TOAST THE MUFFINS.

5. SET A PIECE OF BACON (OR SALMON) ON EACH MUFFIN-HALF.

6. BREAK THE EGGS, ONE AT A TIME, INTO A SHALLOW BOWL, THEN SLIP THEM INTO THE SIMMERING WATER. COVER THE PAN, OR SPOON THE WATER OVER THE TOPS OF THE EGGS.

7. POACH THE EGGS UNTIL THE WHITES ARE SET AND THE YOLKS HAVE FILMED OVER (ABOUT 3-5 MINUTES). REMOVE THEM WITH A SLOTTED SPOON, AND DRAIN WELL ON PAPER TOWELS. THEN CAREFULLY SET AN EGG ON EACH MUFFIN-HALF.

8. TOP THE EGGS WITH ABOUT 2 TABLESPOONS OF THE HOLLANDAISE SAUCE. NOW YOU HAVE EGGS BENEDICT! SERVE IMMEDIATELY.

—AMANDA

HOLLANDAISE SAUCE

1 STICK BUTTER (8 TABLESPOONS)

3 EGG YOLKS (YOU'LL HAVE TO SEPARATE THE EGGS; ASK AN ADULT TO HELP YOU WITH THIS)

SALT

GROUND WHITE PEPPER

1 TABLESPOON LEMON JUICE, OR MORE TO TASTE

MAKES ABOUT 1 CUP

1. MELT THE BUTTER OVER LOW HEAT UNTIL JUST MELTED.

2. PUT THE EGG YOLKS AND LEMON JUICE IN A MEDIUM-SIZE METAL BOWL. WHISK OVER VERY LOW HEAT (OR YOU CAN USE A DOUBLE BOILER) UNTIL IT'S SLIGHTLY THICKENED. REMOVE FROM HEAT.

3. WHISK IN THE BUTTER A LITTLE AT A TIME. ADD THE SALT, PEPPER, AND A LITTLE MORE LEMON JUICE TO TASTE.

cooking tips
from the chef Girls!

The Chef Girls are looking out for you!
Here are some things you should
know if you want to cook.
(Remember to ask your parents
if you can use knives and the stove!)

1   Tie back long hair so that it won't
    get into the food or in the way as
    you work.

2   Don't wear loose-fitting clothing
    that could drag in the food or
    on the stove burners.

3   Never cook in bare feet or open-toed
    shoes. Something sharp or hot could
    drop on your feet.

4   Always wash your hands before you
    handle food.

5   Read through the recipe before you start. Gather your ingredients together and measure them before you begin.

6   Turn pot handles in so that they won't get knocked off the stove.

7   Use wooden spoons to stir hot liquids. Metal spoons can become very hot.

8   When cutting or peeling food, cut away from your hands.

9   Cut food on a cutting board, not the countertop.

10   Hand someone a knife with the knifepoint pointing to the floor.

11   Clean up as you go. It's safer and neater.

12   Always use a dry pot holder to remove something hot from the oven. You could get burned with a wet one, since wet ones retain heat.

13   Make sure that any spills on the floor are cleaned up right away, so that you don't slip and fall.

14 Don't put knives in clean-up water. You could reach into the water and cut yourself.

15 Use a wire rack to cool hot baking dishes to avoid scorch marks on the countertop.

An Important Message from the Chef Girls!

Some foods can carry bacteria, such as salmonella, that can make you sick. To avoid salmonella, always cook poultry, ground beef, and eggs thoroughly before eating. Don't eat or drink foods containing raw eggs. And wash hands, kitchen work surfaces, and utensils with soap and water immediately after they have been in contact with raw meat or poultry.

mooretimes2: Molly and Amanda

qtpie490: Shawn

happyface: Peichi

BrooklynNatasha: Natasha

JustMac: Justin

G-ma R or GR: Grandma Ruthie

Wuzzup: What's up?

Mwa: smooching sound

G2G: Got To Go

deets: details

b-b: Bye-Bye

brb: be right back

L8R: Later, as in "See ya later!"

g8tor: gator, as in "Later gator!"

LOL: Laughing Out Loud

GMTA: Great Minds Think Alike

j/k: Just kidding

B/C or b-cuz: because

W8: Wait

W8 4 me @: Wait for me at

thanx or **thx:** thanks

sez: says

BK: Big kiss

MAY: Mad about you

RUF2T?: Are you free to talk?

TTUL: Type to you later

E-ya: will e-mail you

LMK: Let me know

GR8: Great

WFM: Works for me

2: to, too, two

C: see

u: you

2morrow: tomorrow

2day: today

VH: virtual hug

BFFL: Best Friends For Life

<3 hearts

:-@ shock

:-P sticking out tongue

%-) confused

:-o surprised

;-) winking or teasing

154